WILL SARA STANLEY EVER GO HOME AGAIN?

The door slammed shut with a harsh finality. Sara trembled in the corner. Her legs wavered and she sank to the floor, where she huddled in the shadows. With a longing so deep it was painful, she thought of Aunt Hetty. Of home. Then a horrible thought struck her. She would never see Aunt Hetty again. She would never go home. Nobody in Avonlea knew where she was. Nobody would come looking for her because Jo Pitts would fool all of them. And Sara would rot here, abandoned and alone in the world.

Double Trouble

Storybook written by

Marlene Matthews

Based on the Sullivan Films Production
written by Marlene Matthews
adapted from the novels of

Lucy Maud Montgomery

A BANTAM SKYLARK BOOK®
NEW YORK · TORONTO · LONDON · SYDNEY · AUCKLAND

Based on the Sullivan Films Production produced by Sullivan Films Inc.
in association with CBC and the Disney Channel with the participation
of Telefilm Canada adapted from Lucy Maud Montgomery's novels.

Teleplay written by Marlene Matthews
Copyright © 1991 by Sullivan Films Distribution, Inc.

This edition contains the complete text
of the original edition.
NOT ONE WORD HAS BEEN OMITTED.

RL 6, 008–012

DOUBLE TROUBLE
A Bantam Skylark Book / published by arrangement with
HarperCollins Publishers Ltd.

PUBLISHING HISTORY
HarperCollins edition published 1994
Bantam edition / September 1994

ROAD TO AVONLEA is the trademark of Sullivan Films Inc.

Skylark Books is a registered trademark of Bantam Books,
a division of Bantam Doubleday Dell Publishing Group, Inc.
Registered in U.S. Patent and Trademark Office and elsewhere.

ISBN 0-553-48123-1

Bantam Books are published by Bantam Books, a division of Bantam Doubleday Dell
Publishing Group, Inc. Its trademark, consisting of the words "Bantam Books" and the
portrayal of a rooster, is Registered in U.S. Patent and Trademark Office and in other
countries. Marca Registrada. Bantam Books, 1540 Broadway, New York, New York 10036.

PRINTED IN THE UNITED STATES OF AMERICA
OPM 0 9 8 7 6 5 4 3 2 1

Chapter One

Sara was dreaming—a gentle, lovely sort of dream in which she floated like a feather borne by the wind, weightless, high above the clouds. She smiled to herself, happily dozing. Everything would be perfect—if only her toes weren't so cold.

Instinctively she snuggled down, tugging at the patchwork quilt Aunt Hetty had fashioned for her birthday and pulling it up under her chin for warmth. But her feet were still freezing.

She pulled again, but the quilt stubbornly refused to budge. Had she grown overnight... or had the quilt shrunk? Sara resolved to register a complaint with Aunt Hetty first thing in the morning. After all, how was a person supposed to sleep when her toes were turning to icicles?

Suddenly a sharp sound pierced her dream. Something whisked and scrabbled across her cheek. Sleepily she brushed at her face, longing to drift back to the sweetness of her dream, but the noise persisted. The gentle breeze began to feel damp and chill. Once again she groped for the quilt. This time, however, she was half awake and, with a sudden shock, she realized there was no quilt—her fingers were clutching at thin air!

She opened her eyes and let them adjust to the dim light. Then, with a horrified gasp, she realized what had happened.

She wasn't in her feather bed at Rose Cottage! She was on a filthy dirt floor in a miserably cold room, staring into the beady eyes of a rat, its nose twitching, its whiskers flicking mere inches from her face!

A scream caught in her throat. She sat bolt upright, her heart pounding like a sledgehammer. Her hand touched something cold...a tin pail. In one swift motion she hurled it at the rat. The pail missed and hit the wall with a great clatter. The rat scrabbled and scurried across the floor, disappearing into a hole.

Sara looked around in a panic, suddenly remembering rough hands throwing her into this hovel of a room, voices shouting at her— "That'll learn ye, Jo Pitts!"—then the door bolting shut as she screamed, pounding the walls for help. She recalled the same harsh voices arguing into the night, then an ominous silence as she huddled in the corner, finally crying herself to sleep.

With an awful rush of guilt she thought of the foolish bargain she had struck with Jo Pitts, the ragamuffin Felix swore was her double. It had seemed so innocent, such a lark! The two girls would simply trade places long enough for Sara to take a brief vacation from Aunt Hetty's strict rules and regulations. Sara pictured Jo Pitts snugly ensconced in Rose Cottage, sipping a cozy cup of hot chocolate with Aunt Hetty.

The kitchen would be softly lit, a delicious smell wafting from a freshly baked plum pie cooling on the rack. And from outside, the fragrance of roses and newly mown hay would drift through the kitchen window framed with crisply starched curtains.

Tears brimmed in Sara's eyes and spilled over, running hotly down her cheeks. How could she have been such a fool, running away from the dearest place in the world, from home, from all that was safe and secure? With a desperate yearning, she longed for the sound of Aunt Hetty's voice. How could she have fled willy-nilly, without a care in the world for Aunt Hetty's feelings? And Gus Pike. She had no more considered him than the man in the moon! With anguish, she remembered how she had finagled her way onboard ship, selfishly convincing Gus to take her with him on his quest to find Captain Crane. She recalled trudging with Gus through the winding streets of the city, the sign of The Black Parrot suddenly emerging from thick, dense fog....And with a sick feeling in the pit of her stomach, she thought of that last glimpse of Gus...frightened, pale, fallen into Abe Pike's murderous hands. A sob caught in her throat. Was it only last night? It felt like weeks, months. Time had vanished.

She was a prisoner. There was no escape from this filthy, foul-smelling cell. And they had called her Jo Pitts! Was that why they'd locked her up? They had mistaken her for Jo! What awful crime had Jo Pitts committed to deserve imprisonment? In despair, Sara stared at her hands. They were raw and bleeding where she had scraped them, pounding against the rough wooden door in a desperate attempt to flee. Her dress was ripped and filthy, her stockings torn and streaked with dirt, and her stomach grumbled with hunger.

Just then a glimmer of light caught her attention—daylight, creeping in pale fingers across the floor. She hadn't noticed it the night before, but there was a window, high and narrow and boarded over with a wooden slat. If she could reach it, maybe...just maybe...

Quickly she shoved the pail beneath the window and, standing on tiptoe, she tugged at the board nailed across the frame. With a creak, it gave way. She froze, glancing nervously back at the bolted door. All was silent. Frantically now, she seized the wooden board and swung it with all her might at the window, leaping back as the pane smashed to smithereens. Winding her sash around her hand for protection, she knocked out the remaining jagged bits of glass clinging to the frame, then hoisted herself up and desperately tried to squeeze through the narrow opening.

The sound of the iron bolt slipping its latch stopped her cold. The door flew open and a gangly, pockmarked boy lunged for her as she tried to shinny up the wall. Kicking and screaming, she tried to escape from his grasp, but he threw her to the floor.

"Buck!" he yelled. "Come quick, she's tryin' to give us the slip!"

With a clatter of thick black boots, Buck Hogan stormed into the room, trailed by a gaggle of runny-nosed young boys, all of them dressed in filthy rags and tatters. Sara backed into a corner as Buck loomed over her, his arms crossed, his bowler hat tipped back on his head. Lighting a fat cigar, he smiled amiably.

"Well, now," he said, blowing a smelly cloud of smoke into her face. "Goin' somewheres, Jo Pitts?"

"I'm *not* Jo Pitts!" cried Sara, but this only set off a round of harsh laughter.

"She lost her memory," sneered Rat, the pockmarked boy. He circled her warily as he wiped his nose on the back of his sleeve. "Ain't that a cryin' shame? Makes ye wonder what else she can't remember."

"Yeah, like the money," crowed Mole, a filthy creature whose eyes glittered from a face so grubby it surely hadn't seen soap and water in a month of Sundays.

"What money?" said Sara, struggling to her feet and backing up against the wall.

"The money you stole from me," answered Buck Hogan as he blew a ring of smoke into the air and tossed his hat through the circle. "An' you'll return every penny of it, Jo Pitts, or my name ain't Buck Hogan."

"But I'm telling you, I'm not Jo Pitts, I'm Sara Stanley, and I never stole anything from anybody in my life!" pleaded Sara. "You've made a terrible mistake, Mr. Hogan!"

"Mister?" roared Mole, doubling over with laughter. "She got real fancy since she took off with our loot, eh? *Mister* Hogan! How's that fer a little cheat, eh, *Mister* Hogan?"

"But I'm not a cheat!" cried Sara, setting off another round of derision as the others joined Mole, howling with delight, bowing and scraping around Buck, doffing their caps and whining "*Mister* Hogan, if ye please."

Buck took a sharp whack at Mole and sent him reeling against the wall. The boys fell silent, instantly respectful. Buck threw his cigar to the floor and ground it under his heel. Then he spun around and seized a terrified Sara by the collar.

"Listen hard, Jo Pitts. I had enough o' yer yap. Ye'll pay back what ye stole from me by stealin' some more."

"Stealing...?" Sara's eyes widened in horror. "Oh, Mr. Hogan, you've got it all wrong! I couldn't steal...I wouldn't...!"

"Betcha anything she's got a stash hidden on her right now," crowed Mole, turning out Sara's pockets and retrieving some coins. "What'd I tell ye, Bucko, here's her first payment!" He handed the coins over to Buck, who counted them carefully and shoved them into his own pocket.

"This don't let ye offa the hook, Jo Pitts," sneered Buck. "Tomorrow morning we put ye back to work."

With that he spat on his bowler and carefully dusted it off with a grimy kerchief. "Rat. Mole," he ordered, slapping the bowler on his head and blowing his nose hard in the kerchief before knotting it around his neck. "Board up the window. And do it good, no mistakes." He headed for the door, then stopped to cast a threatening look at Sara, who was in the corner, too frightened to utter a sound. "Don't try nothin' smart, Jo Pitts. You're where ye belong, an' this time it's for keeps."

The door slammed shut with a harsh finality. Sara trembled in the corner. Her legs wavered and she sank to the floor. With a longing so deep it was painful, she thought of Aunt Hetty, of home. Then a horrible thought struck her. She would never see Aunt Hetty again. She would never go home. Nobody in Avonlea knew where she was. Nobody would come looking for her, because Jo Pitts would fool all of them. And Sara would rot here, abandoned and alone in the world.

Chapter Two

The sun shone brightly overhead, but scarcely a ray of light crept into the murky shadows of Twister Lane. In this foul-smelling alley, a ghostly fog crept over the cobblestones and the wind howled like a banshee and echoed off the moldy walls. A mangy dog sniffed at the garbage piled on the road, knocking over tins and tearing at old bones for a shred of meat. At the end of the lane was a filthy hovel, where the wind moaned eerily against a creaking sign. Its faded lettering, barely legible beneath years of grime, read: The Black Parrot.

An innocent traveler happening upon this place would shudder, presuming The Black Parrot to be abandoned, perhaps dangerous... certainly a place to be avoided. He would shiver, turning up his collar against a sudden chill, then beat a hasty retreat to fresh air and sunshine, unable to imagine anything but the devil surviving in such a forbidding spot.

But behind the bolted front door of The Black Parrot, in a back room piled high with old barrels and ropes, lay Gus Pike, chained like a dog to the leg of the bed. And he wasn't alone. His father was with him. Abraham Pike, escaped convict and murderer, was the one man Gus Pike hated and feared with a burning passion, the man who had fought Gus in a fit of jealous rage over Captain Crane and tumbled from the lighthouse into a watery grave.

But the sea had not held Abe Pike in its green tentacles for long. At that very moment, he hovered over his son with a bowl of hot soup, pretending fatherly solicitude and attempting to spoon-feed the boy. Gus turned away. Abe Pike forced the spoon between the boy's lips, but Gus spat in his face. In a rage, Abe hurled the bowl against the wall; then, reining in his temper, he managed a simpering smile.

"Now, son," he whined, his gold tooth glinting in the lamplight, "you gotta keep up your strength. How're ye gonna be any use to me if ye turn into a lily-livered weakling?"

Gus remained stony silent, his face to the wall.

"Is that how ye treat your old man?" Abe moaned. "An' you not seein' me for such a long time!"

"I wouldn't come to see you if you was drawin' your dyin' breath," muttered Gus.

Abe feigned shock. "Now, now, my very own flesh an' blood!" Then he knelt with his ugly face mere inches from Gus's own. "Ye almost got yer wish, my boy. When I fell from that lighthouse in Avonlea into the briny, ye thought I was dead, didn't ye?" He didn't wait for Gus to reply. "Well, I tricked ye. I come back." He fingered an ugly scar running the length of his cheek. "Crane left me a souvenir. Pretty, ain't it?" He grasped the boy's face and forced him to look. "It's vengeance I swore then, an' it's vengeance I'll have. But this time, my boy, you're going to help me."

"I wouldn't lift a finger to help you," said Gus bitterly.

"Ye *will!*" stormed Abe Pike. Then, his voice lowered, his foul breath reeking in Gus's face, "You'll lead me to Ezekiel Crane an' the treasure he's hidin'."

"I ain't leadin' you noplace," retorted Gus boldly. "Captain Crane's my friend an' I ain't betrayin' him fer the likes o' you!"

"You'll tell me where he's hidin'," said Abe, taking off the thick leather belt from around his waist. "You'll tell *me* where he is, or you ain't tellin' *nobody*."

He wound the belt around his fist and moved towards Gus.

Outside in the alley, all was silent except for the creaking of the sign and the harsh thwack of the belt descending. The dog, in the midst of tearing apart a rancid chunk of meat, glanced up and whined. Then it dropped the meat and scurried down the alley with its tail between its legs.

Chapter Three

With great trepidation, Felix helped Jo Pitts load up a tray of glasses and a pitcher of freshly squeezed lemonade.

"Are you sure you know what you're doing?" he asked Jo. "Those ladies out there are sharp as tacks. One wrong move and the jig is up!"

Jo grimaced at him. "Quit bellyaching," she muttered, "and get out of my way."

Felix flew to open the door. Jo Pitts was the picture of innocence as she emerged from Rose Cottage, precariously balancing the tray of frosty glasses and the pitcher of lemonade.

Hetty King was entertaining two of the ladies from the Missionary Society, Mrs. Tarbush and Mrs. Spencer, who were rocking peacefully on the porch, fanning themselves in the warm sunshine and eagerly awaiting a glass of cool, refreshing lemonade.

"Lovely to see you, Sara dear," simpered Fanny Tarbush. "You're growing so nice and tall!"

"Thank you kindly," murmured Jo Pitts, rather enjoying playing the good, sweet child. It was easy fooling these old biddies, especially when she was dressed up in Sara's favorite blue ruffled smock. There were moments when Jo almost believed she really *was* Sara. She glanced back at Felix and smirked.

"Such a darling child," said Mrs. Spencer,

admiring how nicely Sara spoke, "and so well mannered."

Hetty raised an eyebrow. Sara had been anything but well mannered of late. Still, a compliment was a compliment and must be acknowledged. "Yes," she muttered dryly, "she *can* be sweet when she puts her mind to it...."

Jo Pitts wasn't listening. She was mesmerized by the glint of a gold watch pinned to Mrs. Spencer's jacket. A bauble like that would fetch a pretty penny in the city! She looked briefly at Felix, who was nervously hovering near the door. Then she took a breath. Without batting an eyelash, she craftily tipped the pitcher of lemonade, spilling it down the front of Mrs. Spencer's jacket. The startled lady leapt up with a shriek. Felix's eyes almost popped out of his head.

"Good Lord, Sara Stanley!" cried Hetty. "Look what you've done! Get a cloth, and sponge off that jacket at once! I'm dreadfully sorry, Mrs. Spencer. Do let me help you."

"Oh no, it's nothing," sighed Mrs. Spencer, "nothing at all, just a little accident."

"Sorry I wrecked your outfit," said Jo Pitts

with a gush of innocent sweetness, dabbing away at the jacket with a linen napkin.

"Now, now, you dear thing. You mustn't shed a tear over it" was Mrs. Spencer's sympathetic reply. "I'm sure you didn't do it on purpose."

"Oh no!" breathed Jo. "I would never do a thing like that! I'll tell you what. I'll just run and make some more lemonade—how's that?"

Smiling angelically, Jo Pitts toddled off into the house, sweeping past an astounded Felix and leaving the ladies chattering away behind her. She paused in the open doorway, waving politely.

"Wait up!" cried Felix. "I'll come and help."

"Wouldn't think of it!" murmured Jo, allowing the door to slam in his face.

Once alone in the coolness of the hallway, Jo leaned against the door and a wicked smile lit up her face. Clutched in her fist was Mrs. Spencer's lovely little gold watch.

Chapter Four

Warm sunshine drifted down through the trees, white with blossoms, and bathed the church in its clean, fresh light. The ladies of Avonlea, attired in their Sunday best, gathered on the front steps, trading bits of gossip before services began.

Hetty King smoothed her starched skirt and adjusted her spanking-fresh white gloves as her eyes roved the crowd for Sara. Catching sight of the child, dressed in her neatly pressed blue-and-white-striped pinafore and white straw hat, talking quietly to Felix King, Hetty breathed a sigh of relief. For the moment, Sara was behaving herself, and Hetty could safely indulge in her favorite pastime, which was giving her valuable opinion on any subject that arose. Right now, she could hardly wait for Mrs. Sloane to stop moaning and groaning about misplacing her silver sugar tongs.

"Mrs. Sloane," advised Hetty, "misplacing your sugar tongs is not the end of the world. If you retrace your steps and think back to when you last used them, then I assure you that's right where they'll be."

"But they're not, Hetty, I looked!" wailed Mrs. Sloane. "And not only that, my silver sugar bowl is gone too. I'm sure I left them right on the table after Sunday supper!"

"Well, don't that beat all!" sympathized Mrs. Spencer. "I had something go missing too! My gold watch. I had it pinned right to my jacket and poof! It was gone!" She opened her purse to take out a tiny lace-edged handkerchief and dabbed delicately at her nose, leaving her purse hanging open.

From her perch on the steps, Jo Pitts looked sharply at the gaping purse. Drawn as if by a magnet, she began edging slowly towards Mrs. Spencer, all the while keeping up a running patter with an unsuspecting Felix.

Mrs. Bugle wagged her head, a serious expression on her robust face. "That ain't all, ladies. I hear tell Rachel Lynde's good damask tablecloth just plain disappeared off her clothes-line! She's madder than a wet hen about it."

"We're not safe in our beds these days," avowed Mrs. Spencer, with a sober shake of her head.

"I never thought I'd see the day when we'd have to lock our doors in Avonlea," said Hetty.

"It makes me very sad," agreed Mrs. Spencer, completely unaware that Jo Pitts was slyly reaching out a hand to dip into her purse.

Olivia Dale chose that precise moment to smile a greeting to Jo, who snatched back her hand as though a snake had bitten it.

"Sara!" said Olivia warmly. "I haven't seen you for a while. No hello for me, dear?"

"Quick!" whispered Felix, nudging Jo in the ribs. "That's Aunt Olivia. Say hello."

"Hello, Aunt Olivia," parroted Jo Pitts. "Seems like I got so many aunts I can't keep 'em straight."

Olivia looked at her oddly. "You don't have *that* many, Sara."

"She's just joking," said Felix weakly. "Right, Sara?"

Convinced that any moment now Olivia

would spot the imposter, Felix grabbed Jo's arm and hastily steered her up the steps and into the church. Olivia stared after them, unsure what to think.

"Never mind, Olivia," murmured Janet King. "Felix is forever telling bad jokes."

"Yes," said Felicity, "and we don't think they're a bit funny."

"The point is, you just have to grin and bear it until they grow out of it," confided Janet, who was the voice of authority on the habits and oddities of children. Somewhat relieved, Olivia smiled and followed Janet and her brood into church.

"O come, let us sing unto the Lord: let us heartily rejoice in the strength of our salvation," the minister intoned. Above him, sunlight from the stained-glass windows gleamed on his bald head and illuminated the good folk of Avonlea at prayer.

Jo Pitts sat wedged uncomfortably between Hetty and Felix. She poked Hetty in the side and whispered loudly, "Hey...what's he blabbering about?"

Hetty pursed her lips primly, aghast at this outburst. "Bite your tongue!" she muttered.

But to no avail. Jo Pitts merely persisted. "Don't he ever stop? How long's a person supposed to sit here? My bum's gettin' sore!" And with that, she jumped up to leave.

Furious, Hetty yanked her back, and she landed on the seat with a thud. Hetty gritted her teeth until her jaw ached. This was the living end! She must speak to Sara after church and lay down the law once and for all.

"You sit still, young lady, or I'll know the reason why!"

Hetty looked straight ahead, hoping nobody else had noticed the ruckus. Her hand was firmly gripping Sara's wrist lest the child make another move.

Jo Pitts was about to object vociferously, but suddenly her mouth clamped shut. A gleaming brass collection plate, filled to the brim with coins, was being passed down the rows of worshippers. Transfixed by the sight of all that beautiful money, she settled back in her seat, her eyes narrowing craftily. It was too good to be true! She hadn't seen a prize like this since she'd arrived in Avonlea. The wheels were turning in her brain. Everyone staring straight ahead, a church full of old biddies ... and Felix watching her every move! Should she dare? She couldn't resist the challenge. If she was quick about it, this would be like taking candy from a baby!

As the brass plate reached Jo, Felix caught her eye. Ignoring him, she deftly tipped the plate and palmed a great handful of coins into her lace handkerchief before anyone could notice. Smiling sweetly, she tied the handkerchief into a knot and, pretending to scratch her head, slipped it under her straw hat. Then she passed the plate to Hetty, who glanced at the half-empty plate and added a good-sized donation. Jo Pitts rolled her eyes heavenward and joined in the singing of "Amazing Grace" louder than any God-fearing member of the congregation.

Once outside the church and out of earshot of Aunt Hetty and his mother, who were milling around discussing their Sunday dinner menus, Felix cornered Jo Pitts.

"I saw what you did!" he whispered, outraged. "You stole that money. I saw you stick it under your hat! Give it back this minute or I'm *telling!*"

Jo Pitts responded by hauling off and shoving him backwards. Caught off balance, he stumbled. Then, scrambling to his feet again, he made a lunge for her hat. The hat went flying, the lace handkerchief tumbled out, and coins spilled and clanked down the cement steps.

Hetty whipped about in astonishment. Now, in Hetty King's experience, two and two always made four; therefore, when she saw the money, coupled with Felix's frightened look and Sara's wide-eyed innocence, she leapt to an unshakable conclusion. With a grave "Hmph!" she confronted her sister-in-law.

"I don't know how this happened, Janet King," she said accusingly, "but with Felix's help, it seems the money from the collection plate has ended up in Sara's possession!"

"I beg your pardon?" was Janet's horrified reply. "What do you mean with Felix's help?"

"You don't think Sara thought this up all by herself, do you?" said Hetty, with a disapproving glare at Felix, who almost choked. "Return this money to the minister, and be quick about it, *both of you!*"

Hetty and Janet watched, thin-lipped with anger and flushed with embarrassment, as the children handed over the coins to the minister.

"This settles it, Janet King," said Hetty coldly. "Felix is a dreadfully bad influence on Sara and I think it best if they don't play together in the future."

"Oh you do, do you!" retorted Janet, another rush of color reddening her cheeks. "Well, I think it's the other way around! It's Sara who eggs Felix on. But if that's the way you want it, so be it!" With that, she seized Felix by the scruff of the neck. "Felix, let's go! We're not staying where we're not wanted."

Dragging a bewildered Felix behind her, Janet marched across the churchyard past the curious eyes of her neighbors. In a huff, Hetty took Sara's hand firmly in her own and stalked off in the opposite direction. Had she bothered to glance down at the young girl trotting along beside her, she would have noted a most unangelic smirk on Jo Pitts' face.

Chapter Five

Felix King was miserable. He sat at the kitchen table, staring longingly at the delectable leftovers, roast beef and cinnamon-apple pie, resting on platters mere inches from his face. He knew if he dared lift a fork to steal a crumb of pie while his mother was lecturing him, she would be more furious than ever.

"I want the truth, Felix King. Who took that money? Was it you?"

The dreaded question. Felix squirmed, wishing he were on the moon instead of in the King farm kitchen. If he said yes, he'd be punished. If he said no, he might still be punished because nobody would believe him. Moreover, telling the truth would endanger Sara Stanley's escapade, and he had promised faithfully he would protect her secret, no matter what.

"No" was his anguished reply. "It wasn't me."

"Well, if it wasn't you, was it Sara?" insisted Janet.

Felix groaned. Perhaps if he responded with a partial truth, his mother would be satisfied and the whole matter would evaporate into thin air. "It wasn't exactly Sara," he said, with his fingers crossed behind his back.

"Who was it, then?" demanded Janet.

Felix was stuck. He bit his lip and remained silent.

"I'm speaking to *you*, young man!" Janet looked deep into her son's eyes, and Felix wished the floor would open up and swallow him. Still, he maintained his silence.

This was too much. Janet stood up. "Until I hear the truth," she announced, "it's bread and milk for your dinner." She removed the platter of roast beef and the fragrant apple pie from the table. He watched it go with imploring eyes. His stomach gurgled with hunger and there was nothing he could do but sit there silently while the mouth-watering delicacies vanished.

Life wasn't fair. There was Sara Stanley off on a silly lark of a holiday and he was stuck in Avonlea with Jo Pitts and bread and milk for supper. He hoped Sara appreciated the serious sacrifices he was making in the name of friendship and cousinhood!

Jo Pitts wasn't suffering any such moral dilemma. Far from it. While Hetty King harangued and interrogated her, she was blithely juggling a couple of apples in the air, as carefree as one could imagine.

"Put those apples back in the bowl!" snapped Aunt Hetty. "And sit still while I'm talking to you!"

Jo put the apples back on the table and they rolled to the floor, so she grabbed two more from the bowl and began to toss them around as though Hetty hadn't spoken a word.

"I said *put those down!*"

When Jo Pitts ignored her, she began to pace feverishly.

"Never in the entire history of the King family has there been a thief!" sputtered Hetty. "And now you! Ruth's child! I am thoroughly humiliated. What have I done wrong? Where were your brains, girl? Letting Felix King get you into such a scrape!"

Jo Pitts looked up at her with eyes like saucers. "I know it don't look too good."

"It *doesn't*," corrected Aunt Hetty.

"Yep, it sure don't, you got that right," agreed Jo, munching heartily on one of the apples.

"Then why on earth did you do it?" wailed Hetty, thoroughly perplexed by Sara's behavior.

"Oh... " said Jo slowly, cradling her head in her hands and moaning softly, "I guess it was on accounta my head hurtin' so much."

"Your head...?" said Hetty, suddenly worried. "Why are you holding your head? What's bothering you?"

"I get these awful pains..."

"Good Lord!" Hetty's hand flew to her lips. "You don't mean you're...sick...?"

"Oh yeah," agreed Jo, "that's it. Sick as a dog."

Instantly filled with remorse, Hetty stared at the young girl who just a moment before had looked the picture of health. "Sara dear, why in heaven's name didn't you tell me before?"

"'Cuz the voices told me not to," replied Jo Pitts.

"The voices? *What* voices?"

"The ones in my head," said Jo innocently. "Don't you never hear no voices?"

Hetty gasped. "Lord in heaven, *no!* You poor dear soul, how long have you been hearing voices?"

"Since I had the fever," said Jo lightly.

Hetty racked her brain to remember Sara ever having a fever. "This is terrible," she said, her voice shaking. "I've been so busy teaching you manners and giving you lessons, I never noticed your state of health! Oh, you poor child. I've neglected you! This is all my fault! Let me make you some camomile tea."

"Sure," said Jo. "And what's for supper?"

"Well, at least you have an appetite! That's a very good sign." Hetty fussed over Jo, gently smoothing back her blond hair. "Yes. Good food and plenty of rest, that's what you need. I'll make whatever your little heart desires. Anything at all. Just say the word."

"I'll have cake," said Jo.

"Cake...?" Then, frightened of aggravating Sara's mysterious condition, Hetty quickly added, "Of course you can have cake. Cake is nourishing. What kind would you like?"

"Oh, chocolate, double layer, strawberry icing," said Jo, putting her feet up on the table and scratching her ears.

Hetty choked back her feelings and managed a weak smile. Nobody had ever put dirty shoes on *her* table. Still, Sara wasn't well, and if she reprimanded the child, heaven knew what course her illness might take.

"I'll make it right away," she said meekly. "You just sit there quietly."

Jo Pitts leaned back comfortably in her chair and watched Hetty bustle about the kitchen in her rush to make a double-layer chocolate cake. For a brief moment Jo wondered if she should have demanded more...perhaps apple pie with whipped cream on top, or plum pudding with vanilla sauce, or even a tangy lemon curd with brown sugar drizzling lazily down the sides.... Then she thought better of it. Order up more tasty treats tomorrow, more the day after, that was the plan! Keep Miss Hetty-know-it-all-King too busy to think straight, too addled to notice what was going on right under her nose!

Jo Pitts chortled gleefully. Without half trying, she had found the soft spot in Hetty's shriveled-up heart. Pretend you're sick and the old bat would melt like a pat of butter in the summer sun. Well, now, thought Jo, as Hetty rattled pots and pans and mixing bowls in her haste to prepare the chocolate cake, this is more like it. Livin' here with the old bat might not be so bad after all!

Chapter Six

The alley was dark and silent. Shadows crept up dank walls, signaling the setting of a wan sun, when suddenly the clatter of rough footsteps on cobblestones shattered the silence. Buck Hogan's burly figure emerged from the darkness, dragging Sara Stanley behind him.

"Get a move on," he snarled, roughly yanking her arm. "I ain't got all day!"

She stumbled along, peering into the misty darkness in hopes of getting her bearings, desperately seeking a chance to bolt and run.

Then all at once, Buck Hogan made a swift turn into yet another narrow alleyway and Sara gasped. This was Twister Lane...the very place she and Gus had sought in the quest for Captain Crane! Was it possible? Was Buck Hogan in cahoots with Abraham Pike? Before she had time to think about what this might mean, a gust of wind gathered force and howled eerily down the lane. She could hear the creaking of the sign, the dreaded mark of The Black Parrot.

"Aye, and we're here," muttered Buck as the mist parted and the rusty sign became visible to the naked eye.

Sara could barely breathe. "Please let Gus Pike still be there," she murmured to herself, her fists clenched tightly. Then her heart gave a fearful lurch. When she had last seen Gus, he'd been struggling to get away from Abe Pike. What if he had failed? Abraham Pike was an escaped convict, a murderer—he might have kidnapped Gus, harmed him! A sixth sense warned her to remain silent as Buck pounded heavily on the thick wooden door.

"Open up!" he yelled. "It's me an' Jo Pitts come to see ye."

After an awful silence, the door swung open.

"Well, ain't this somethin'!" whined a guttural voice. It was Abraham Pike, holding up an oil lamp, the flame illuminating the angry red scar raked across his cheek. "It's Jo Pitts, come back from the dead!" he declared. Then his eyes narrowed and the smile vanished. "We got some talkin' to do." With a quick look at Buck Hogan, he reached out a gnarled hand and seized Sara, drawing her inside. With a thud, the great wooden door closed behind them.

Except for the smoky flicker of the oil lamp, they were in pitch darkness. The smell was vile, a rotting dampness mixed with stale food and garbage. She shrank back into the shadows, watching, waiting, praying Gus Pike was alive.

Buck and Abe Pike muttered in harsh tones to one another. "There she was, runnin' around plain as day," explained Buck, proud of his captive, "so I nabbed her an' brought her straight to ye!"

"And a good thing ye did!" was Abe Pike's reply. "The little guttersnipe owes me money." He peered into Sara's face, his gold tooth gleaming in the lamplight. "Friends what runs out on us ain't friends no more, eh, Jo Pitts?"

His face was so close Sara could smell the tobacco and whiskey on his breath. Her heart pounded fearfully as a growling dog brushed by her legs. Abraham Pike continued talking, unaware that Sara was staring at something over his shoulder. Now the dog was whining and scratching at a door that Sara could barely make out in the darkness of the room. Pike's harangue continued. The dog nudged the door open and crept inside, leaving the door ajar.

Sara stifled a gasp of horror, for there was Gus Pike, curled up on the floor. He was bruised and battered, more dead than alive. His leg was still chained to the bed. For a brief moment their eyes met, both stunned and grateful to see one other alive. Then quickly Gus motioned to Sara to be silent.

"Are ye deaf?" snarled Abe Pike, seizing her by the throat. "I'm talkin' to ye! Did ye come back to return the money ye stole?"

Sara felt his rough hands around her neck. His eyes burned into hers. She tried desperately not to flinch.

"Oh, she did, she brung ye this," said Buck Hogan, hastily handing over the coins he had taken from Sara's pocket. "Just to show her heart's in the right place, boss."

"This all of it?" demanded Abe Pike, greedily counting the hoard of coins and shoving them into his pocket.

"Fer starters," said Buck, glaring at Sara. "Ain't that so?"

Sara looked from one to the other in frightened silence.

"Speak up!" ordered Buck. "The boss asked ye a question."

"Oh!" gasped Sara. "Yes sir, sorry sir."

"Sir, is it!" declared Abe Pike with a pleased smile. He leaned back with his arms folded. "Seems ye learned respect since ye flew the coop. I likes respect."

"Yes sir," murmured Sara, trying her hardest to distract Abe Pike and at the same time not to look through the doorway where poor Gus lay in chains.

"Then remember this," Abe Pike warned, his anger sparking like a flash of lightning, "the next time ye runs out on us, ye'll end up in the boneyard!"

"She ain't runnin' noplace, boss. I'm keepin'

my eye on her, don't you worry none," boasted Buck Hogan. "She'll pay up every penny. I'm startin' her to work right off, I swear it!"

"Then out with ye," roared Pike, "afore I chops yer heads in a bucket an' feeds ye to the sharks!" With that he flung the front door open and shoved the two of them outside.

Sara whirled around and caught one final glimpse of Gus Pike before the door crashed shut.

Moments later, Buck Hogan was rushing her down Twister Lane. They were swallowed up in inky darkness, and only the wind and the creaking sign of The Black Parrot were witnesses to Sara's plight.

Gus Pike bided his time. He knew Abe Pike like the back of his hand; there was only one way to avoid his violent temper and that was to give the old scoundrel what he wanted. And what Abe Pike wanted was Captain Ezekiel Crane's head on a silver platter...along with the treasure he imagined Crane had hidden away beyond Pike's greedy reach.

Now that Gus knew Sara Stanley was alive, he was determined to rescue her from Buck

Hogan's grasp. He had to break free. A plan began to take shape in his head. He waited silently, patiently, until Pike brought in a bowl of watery soup for his dinner.

"There ye be, my boy. Will ye eat it tonight or do I give it to the dog?"

"I'll eat it," said Gus.

"Well, well!" mocked Abe. "An' to what do I owe this honor?"

"Nothin'," said Gus quietly. "Only I want to know something. Where'd you find the girl?"

"Jo Pitts?" said Abe, raising a spoonful of soup to Gus's lips.

Gus swallowed the vile concoction and breathed a sigh of relief. Who in tarnation was Jo Pitts? Never mind. If Abe thought Sara was Jo, all the better. Perhaps this mistake would buy Sara time, valuable time, time during which Gus might win his freedom and rescue her from her captors. Not a flicker of emotion crossed his face as he obediently swallowed the soup and continued talking to Abe.

"Yeah," said Gus, "that's the one, Jo Pitts. She took money from me. I got a score to settle with her."

Abe Pike roared with laughter. "You don't seem to have much luck, my boy! Taken in by the likes of Jo Pitts. Tricked by a villain like Ezekiel Crane!"

"We all make mistakes, Pa," said Gus carefully.

"Ain't it the truth," agreed Abe Pike, pleased as punch to have his rebellious son confess a failing. "Ye've been diddled by the best, my boy!"

"I only want what's comin' to me, Pa," Gus muttered, knowing his father would rise to the bait. "I don't blame you for bein' mad at me. I shoulda told ya everything right from the start."

"Well, it ain't too late," whined Abe. "After all, I'm yer pa. I got forgiveness in my heart."

"Then maybe it's time we gave each other a hand," offered Gus. "I'll tell you what. If you'll help me get my money back from Jo Pitts, I'll help you find Captain Crane."

Abe could hardly believe his ears. After refusing over and over to reveal a word of Crane's whereabouts, Gus was finally willing to relent? Jo Pitts must have rankled the boy good and proper, for as much as Abe Pike hated the little devil, it appeared Gus hated her more.

"Course, I can't lead you to Crane if I'm in chains, Pa."

Abe loomed over his son. He loosened the keys from his belt, then hesitated. For an awful moment, Gus sucked in his breath, fearing the ruse had failed.

"I guess you'll want to know the secret," Gus said, looking around carefully as though the walls had ears.

"I wasn't about to set ye free without gettin' nothin' in return'," snarled Abe.

"Then here it is." Gus lowered his voice confidentially. "Captain Crane's hiding in Jamaica. He won't talk to nobody but me, so I'll have to take you to him."

For a split second, Abe stared at him, unsure. He had hoped to worm Crane's whereabouts from the boy and then leave him here to rot. Still, he thought bitterly, it was just like Crane to confide in no one but Gus, just to get Abe Pike's goat. Abe knelt and inserted the key in the padlock on the leg irons. The clasp fell away and Gus rose painfully to his feet.

"Thanks, Pa," he murmured, managing a

small grin before adding, "I guess we're partners now."

"Partners it is, my boy," said Abe Pike, the jagged scar gaping and stretching eerily as he returned the smile.

Now the treasure was so close, thought Abe, he could almost smell it! If he closed his eyes, he could feel the cold, hard sparkle of diamonds, the thrill of rubies and emeralds and sapphires spilling through his fingers. Soon it would be his, the treasure that had eluded him these many long years. Fate works in mysterious ways, marveled Abe. That rotten little Jo Pitts, appearing out of the blue and making Gus so hopping mad he upped and betrayed Ezekiel Crane just to get even! Well, it proved one thing, he thought to himself, blood is thicker than water. Even so, he'd trust Gus about as far as he could throw him. He'd watch him like a hawk. Trick the lad into leading him to Crane and hunt up the treasure—that's the ticket. Then he'd do away with the lot of them, liars and thieves all three—Jo Pitts, Gus Pike and Captain Ezekiel Crane, all cut from the same miserable piece of cloth. First he'd get the treasure, then he'd rid himself of the traitors. Feed 'em to the sharks, that's what.

Chapter Seven

A pale moon shone over Avonlea, casting silvery shadows across the fields and woods. The night air was full of the scent of balsamic fir, borne on the breeze that drifted through the bedroom windows of Avonlea's peacefully sleeping townsfolk.

At Rose Cottage, however, the dark, sweet scent of balsam failed to soothe Hetty King's shattered nerves. In her high-necked pink nightgown, her bedcap pulled over a headful of rag curlers, she tossed and turned in a fitful sleep, beset with strange and terrible nightmares. "No...no...noooo!" she moaned, her arms flailing out into the night as she fended off some nameless terror.

Suddenly a crash from downstairs jolted her awake. She gasped and leapt out of bed, clutching her blankets to her bosom, whirling around to get her bearings. Another tremendous crash!

She stifled a scream and fumbled on the dresser for her hairbrush. Then, brandishing it as a weapon, her heart pounding a mile a minute, she tiptoed out of the room.

For a moment she paused at the head of the stairs, listening, her eyes adjusting to the dark. Then, from under the kitchen door, she noticed a sliver of pale yellow light. Someone...something...was in her kitchen! For a moment all was quiet. Then the sharp *clink-clank* of metal broke the silence, the sound emanating from downstairs, from behind the closed kitchen door!

Gathering her courage, she slipped down the steps, chin jutting out, palms perspiring, determined to stalk the foe, be it human or otherwise, lurking at this very moment in the kitchen of Rose Cottage!

With the hairbrush poised for attack, she peered through a crack in the door. Then she gasped, for there was Sara, in her nightdress, sitting at the kitchen table with all of Hetty's fine silverware laid out before her. One by one she was counting the knives, spoons and forks, a positively demonic look in her eye as she stacked each piece into a neat pile. Hetty's eyes widened. The child was muttering to herself. Hetty strained to hear, but couldn't quite make out the words, something about Huck Bogan, Dogan, Hogan. Hetty could make no sense of it whatsoever. Was the child dreaming, sleep-walking...?

Hetty shoved the door open and barged in. "Sara Stanley!" she exclaimed. "What in God's name are you doing!"

Jo Pitts dropped the fork like a hot potato. "Uh...nothin', Aunt Hetty," she muttered. "Just cleanin' the silver, that's all."

"In the middle of the night?"

"Oh sure," said Jo, spitting on a knife and polishing it with the sleeve of her nightdress.

"Are you *spitting* on my silverware?" shrieked Hetty, shocked at this peculiar clean-ing method. "Where did you ever learn such a dreadful thing!"

"From the voices."

"The...voices?" asked Hetty nervously.

"Yep," said Jo. "I'm layin' in my bed, all covered up tight, sleepin' like a baby, an' I hear 'em. The voices in my head. They nag me somethin' fierce. 'Get up an' spit on the silver, get up an' spit on the silver.' Drives a person crazy, lemme tell ya."

"Good Lord." Hetty stared at her, thoroughly shaken. This was disastrous. The child heard voices in her head telling her to get up and spit on the silver, and she obeyed them? She was ill. Terribly ill. Hetty would have to handle the situation with kid gloves. Lord only knew what the child might do if provoked. Very gingerly, Hetty put down the hairbrush and patted Sara on the shoulder. Mustn't excite her, mustn't alarm her.

"Sara dear," she murmured, desperately trying to sound calm even though she was trembling from head to toe, "just leave the silver where it is, dear heart, and go to bed. I'll bring you up a nice cup of hot chocolate."

"And cake?" said Jo craftily.

"Cake. Of course, cake."

Hetty held her breath while Jo considered the offer. Then Jo beamed up at her, jumped off the chair and headed for the stairs, where she paused to smile wickedly at Hetty.

"Whatcha starin' at, ya old poophead?" she taunted. "Can't ya see I'm starvin'?"

Hetty nodded weakly and managed a tiny wave of her hand. Jo bounded up the stairs, leaving Hetty pale and frozen to the spot, her mind reeling. What was she to do? She needed time...time to think. One wrong move on her part and the dreadful imbalance in the child's brain could tip the wrong way, and...she could only shudder at the awful possibility. She must be resourceful, resolute. No matter how painful, she must do the right thing for poor, dear Sara.

A few minutes later, Hetty was sitting by Sara's bedside, watching her guzzle down the last dregs of hot chocolate from the bottom of the cup. Sara let out an unseemly belch and licked the remaining crumbs of apple crumb cake from the dish. Hetty stared. Such dreadful manners! Not an "excuse me," not a "beg your pardon." Licking the dish like a ragamuffin off the street!

Stifling her customary reprimand, Hetty turned out the light. "Time to sleep, Sara," she murmured, rising, gathering up the tray of dishes and moving quickly towards the door.

Jo bounced under the quilt and turned her head to the wall without the merest glance at Hetty.

"Good night, dear," said Hetty, pausing in the doorway to look back at Sara's blond curls tumbling across the pillow. How could such a well brought up child have turned into such a devil? she thought fearfully. Then she left the room, closing the door behind her.

In the hallway she took a deep breath. Then she took a key from her pocket and carefully locked the door. As she expected, there was a cry of outrage from within the bedroom.

"Hey!" yelled Jo Pitts. "Whatcha lockin' the door for?"

"For your own good," whispered Hetty sadly to herself. She slipped the key back in her pocket. There were tears in her eyes.

Chapter Eight

The next morning, Janet and Olivia tore across the field to Rose Cottage in a state of alarm. Never in all their years of dealing with

King family trials and tribulations had they been summoned to deal with an emergency quite like this one. Even from a distance they could hear the terrible commotion. Sara was screaming like a banshee and her voice rang out across the meadow: "LEMMMEEE OUTTA HERE!"

The two aunts stared at one another in horror.

"Good Lord!" breathed Janet King, her hand fluttering to her lips.

Holding on to their hats, they raced towards the gate, flung it open and stumbled headlong for the front door. Before they could touch the knocker, a bedraggled Hetty opened the door and fell into their arms.

"Thank God you're here!" she cried, ushering them inside. Suddenly, a gigantic crash thundered from upstairs.

Olivia's eyes widened in shock. "Hetty! Are you all right? What on earth is going on up there?"

"It's *her*," Hetty wailed, wringing her hands in desperation. "She's throwing the furniture around."

"But *why?*" exclaimed Olivia, instinctively ducking as another crash exploded overhead.

"Because she's having a...a *fit*. I locked her in her room last night."

"Locked her in?" said an astonished Janet.

"I had to. She got up to spit on the silver at midnight."

"But that's plain crazy!" was Olivia's shocked response.

"I know." Hetty winced at the sound of crashing glass. "And that's not the worst of it. She's sick, poor child! She hears voices in her head."

Janet had to shout to be heard over the screams from upstairs. "Hetty, it sounds as though she's turned into a raving lunatic!"

"Bite your tongue!" snapped Hetty. "There's never been even a hint of lunacy in the King family!"

Suddenly there was dead silence from above. The ladies looked at one another in terror.

"Now what?" whispered Hetty, clutching the bannister and fearing the worst.

"I don't know," Janet whispered back. "But let's not wait to find out what she plans to do next!"

Janet charged for the stairs, followed by Hetty and Olivia tripping over one another in their haste to reach Sara before she harmed herself.

"Now remember," cautioned Hetty as she stumbled up the steps, "don't be too hard on her. Think of the voices! Lord knows what they'll tell her to do!"

At the top of the stairs, Hetty fumbled in her pocket. "The key! Where'd I put the key?"

"Hurry, Hetty!" hissed Olivia. Then she turned to the closed door and called out sweetly, "Sara dearest, it's Aunt Olivia. Stay calm, dear!"

Precious seconds ticked by before Hetty grasped the key and, with trembling fingers, unlocked the door.

Carefully, ever so carefully, Hetty turned the handle and opened the door. She cast a nervous glance at Olivia and Janet. Gingerly, they followed her inside.

Sara's bedroom looked as though it had been struck by a tornado. Books, quilts and clothes were strewn every which way. The gilt-edged mirror that hung above the dressing table was smashed to smithereens and the table itself had been overturned. The feather mattress was ripped and dumped on its side. Clouds of white goose down fluttered airily in a gentle breeze that ruffled the curtains at the open window.

All three ladies gasped, the meaning of the sudden silence dawning on them. Sara Stanley had flown the coop!

"Oh no!" gasped Hetty.

"She can't get far!" cried Janet.

As one, the three ladies lunged for the door, crashing into each other in their haste.

"Pardon me," muttered Olivia.

"Excuse me," murmured Janet.

"This is no time for etiquette!" wailed Hetty. "Hurry, before the child does something terrible!"

All three squeezed past each other, piling downstairs and storming out of the cottage in pursuit of Sara Stanley.

Chapter Nine

The wharf was teeming with people of all kinds going about the daily routine of business. Vendors hawked their wares at colorful stalls filled to overflowing with fresh vegetables, iron pots and pans, lace from Dublin, silks and ivory from the Far East, tobacco and spices from the Indies. Busy housewives with runny-nosed children clutching at their skirts picked and pawed through bushels of polished apples and tomatoes, bargaining for the best prices, while elegantly attired gentlemen and their ladies browsed among the fine silks and satins, whiling away the sunny morning in idle gossip.

Buck Hogan and his pack of thieves surveyed the crowd and set their sights on one particular gentleman who had just made an error...one that singled him out as ripe for the plucking. The fine gent, or "mark," as the gang called a prospective victim, had just retrieved an intricately engraved gold pocket watch from his vest, glanced at it and carelessly put it back...all in full view of Buck Hogan's greedy eyes. In so doing, the mark had sealed his fate, for Buck Hogan coveted that watch. Not for himself, but for the boss, Abe Pike, who required a hefty prize at the end of each working day from his loyal band of pickpockets.

Buck Hogan picked his teeth with a splinter

of wood and eyed the unfortunate gentleman. Satisfied that the watch could be easily grasped by nimble fingers, he nodded to Sara Stanley, who was crouching nervously beside him.

"There ye go, Jo Pitts," he snarled. "Here's yer chance to make amends."

Sara cast him a horrified look. This gang of notorious louts not only thought she was Jo Pitts, but they expected her to steal just as they did! She shrank back, too frightened to move. She wouldn't do it! Steal a watch from a perfectly innocent gentleman? She couldn't!

Almost as though reading her thoughts, Buck Hogan yanked her by the throat and hauled her to her feet. "Ye'll do as yer told, Jo Pitts, or ye'll live to the rue the day ye came back!" And with that, he shoved her into the gentleman's path.

Sara froze. Buck hissed to Rat, who was hovering nearby, "I don't trust her. Stick by her," and the younger lad hastily slithered into the crowd milling around Sara.

Buck then nodded silently to Mole, who sprang into action. The plan was well rehearsed, and Mole was the expert, having successfully carried it to completion on many a morning such as this. The gist of the plan was simple: create a diversion, then pickpocket the mark during the commotion.

To this end, Mole now proceeded to knock over a bushel of apples directly in front of a man riding a bicycle. The bicycle lurched and tipped and the rider went sprawling. In a flash, Mole was kneeling beside him.

"Get a doctor!" yelled Mole, feigning solicitude, all the while pinning down the unfortunate man, who was struggling to his feet and attempting to get back on his bicycle. A crowd quickly gathered to gawk, and in that split second, Buck glared at Sara.

"*Now!*" he ordered. "Do it now, or I tell the boss yer holdin' out on him!"

For an awful moment, Sara considered running, but with Buck and Rat breathing down her neck, she was trapped. The fine gentleman was mere inches from her. Buck watched her every move.

Her heart pounding, she crept slowly towards the gentleman, her hand reaching for his pocket. In a flash, the gold watch was in her fingers. She hesitated...and the moment's hesitation did her in, for the gentleman glanced down and spotted her.

"Help! Constable!" he yelled, seizing Sara by the arm. "I've caught a pickpocket!"

A whistle blew shrilly and a policeman raced towards them, roaring, "Stop! Stop thief!" A look of horror crossed Buck Hogan's face. He fled. Rat and Mole ducked for cover and vanished into the crowd.

Sara's mind raced. It was a chance....She could let the policeman catch her and then go through a long-winded grilling about her identity, and why she was stealing a gold watch. Fine if they believed the truth...but if they didn't, Lord knows what might happen! She might rot in jail, and Gus could lose his life at the hands of Abe Pike. No, she couldn't risk being caught. She had to act and act now!

She looked up at the fine gentleman and whispered, "I'm terribly sorry, Sir. Please forgive me!" Then she kicked the poor man in the shins as hard as she could. He howled with pain and clutched his leg, letting go of her for a fraction of a second. She threw the watch at him, wrenched free and raced pell-mell into the crowd.

"Catch her!" roared the gentleman, hopping up and down on one leg.

The policeman thundered past in pursuit of the blond waif who was running like the wind, dodging pushcarts and bicycles only to disappear round a dark corner.

Buck Hogan caught a flash of the blond hair and signaled to Rat and Mole. "There she goes. Cut her off!" The pack of thieves moved like lightning, hoping to trap Sara at the end of the alley.

She could hear the clatter of feet behind her. Desperately she scanned the alley for a place to hide. In a panic she whirled around, just as a hand reached out and dragged her into a shadowy doorway. A scream rose in her throat, but a rough hand clapped over her mouth, silencing her.

"Shhh! It's me!"

The voice was deep and husky...and familiar. Stunned, she looked up into Gus Pike's eyes.

"Gus!" she blurted out. "How did you get here?"

"Never mind," he whispered. "Do as I say, and don't ask questions." But just as these words were uttered, Sara gasped, for directly behind Gus she saw Buck Hogan and his gang tearing towards them, followed by Abe Pike, who was panting and mopping his brow.

Gus caught the look of terror in her eyes. Instantly he understood. In a flash, his expression changed. Eyes glittering menacingly, he snatched her by the scruff of the neck and held her up like a rat caught in a trap. For the benefit of Abe Pike and Buck Hogan, he sneered at Sara. "So I finally nabbed ya, Jo Pitts!" Then he turned to Buck with a friendly grin. "How ya doin', Bucko? Good thing we caught this little devil, ain't it!"

Chapter Ten

"Leggo o' me, ya old crows!" screamed Jo Pitts as Olivia, Janet and Hetty cornered her behind a clump of bushes. "I didn't do nothin'! An' I ain't goin' back to that ol' witch!"

Hetty King pursed her lips. "I presume she

means me," she said, bewildered and embarrassed by Sara's wild behavior. "A fine how-
do-you-do for all the patience I've shown! My
own niece calling me a witch!"

"You mind your tongue, young lady!"
warned Janet King, seizing Jo Pitts by the arm
and pulling her out of her hiding place. Jo bit
Janet's hand with a vengeance. Screaming,
Janet clutched her hand in pain and Jo broke
loose, kicked Olivia squarely in the bustle and
tore hell for leather across the fields.

Astounded, Olivia hiked up her dainty
skirts and tore after her. "Sara!" she screamed.
"Stop this instant!"

Swiftly, Jo Pitts leapt over a low wooden
fence, but pride was her downfall. She
couldn't resist a triumphant glance back at
Olivia, and she lost her footing, stumbled and
fell. In one swoop, Olivia sailed over the fence
and pounced on her.

"HELP! MURDER!" hollered Jo Pitts, arms
flailing out at her captor.

"No you don't!" gasped Olivia, pinning her
to the ground. "This time I'm putting you
where you can't get out!"

Janet and Hetty looked on nervously as Olivia struggled to drag Jo back over the fence. The girl broke free and Olivia made a dive for her, grasping her firmly around the knees. She slung Jo over her back like a sack of potatoes. Jo squirmed and screamed but Olivia summoned up every ounce of strength, scaled the fence, dumped her inside the outhouse and locked the door.

"There," declared Olivia, leaning against the door for good measure, "that should hold the little devil."

Hetty was doubtful. The bashing and pounding and yelling from within the outhouse would surely rouse the entire countryside. People would ask questions—prying, nasty questions. And how could she ever explain that dear, polite little Sara Stanley had turned into a hellion and had to be locked up for her own safety, not to mention the protection of any hapless soul who crossed her path?

"Open up! It stinks in here!" yelled Jo Pitts.

"Well, I never...!" cried Janet. "Hetty King, how can you allow her to carry on like this!"

"How can I stop her?" wailed Hetty.

"I said open up, you old battleaxes!"

"You'd better get used to it!" Olivia yelled back to the voice from the outhouse, much to Hetty's embarrassment. "Because that's where you're staying until we figure out what to do with you!"

"What *are* we going to do?" whispered Hetty.

"Go suck my elbow!" screamed Jo Pitts, pounding with all her might on the outhouse walls.

"We can't keep her in there forever," whispered Hetty in desperation.

"Why not?" muttered Janet. "She deserves worse."

"I agree!" said Olivia emphatically. Locking up this outrageous child and throwing away the key seemed a perfectly sensible solution just then.

"Maybe we should take turns watching her," Janet suggested. "A vigil, day and night."

"Hot baths," said Hetty nervously, "I read that hot baths are very soothing."

"And a dose of castor oil. Clean her right out," added Janet, retreating from an exceptionally loud smash on the wall.

"And a tonic," Olivia shouted over a series of ear-splitting screams from Jo Pitts. "Twice a day, it settles the nerves!"

"We're deluding ourselves, ladies!" hollered Janet, covering her ears as the crashing and bashing worsened. "A tonic won't settle Sara down! She's a raving maniac. I say call in a specialist from the city!"

"A specialist!" retorted Hetty. "Nonsense! They might tell you what's wrong with your left nostril, but they don't know a thing about the right!"

"Not that kind of specialist!" cried Janet. "I mean one of those newfangled head doctors, someone who'll talk some sense into her!"

"Those idiots!" exclaimed Hetty. "She'd talk rings around them."

Suddenly Jo Pitts let out a long, wild yowl that made it sound as though a horde of tormented alleycats had settled in the King outhouse. This, decided Hetty, was the last straw.

"Ladies," she said leadenly, "there's only one thing to do."

She took Olivia and Janet aside. All three leaned over and whispered in a huddle.

෬෨෬෨

Abe Pike looked into Sara's eyes, his gold tooth
gleaming. "Friends that runs out on us ain't friends
no more, eh Jo Pitts?" His face was so close that Sara
could smell the tobacco and whiskey on his breath.

❧❧❧

"HELP! MURDER!" hollered Jo Pitts, her arms
flailing at her captor. "No you don't!" gasped Olivia.
"This time I'm putting you where you can't get out!"

❧❧❧

Steal a watch from a perfectly innocent stranger?
Sara couldn't! "Ye'll do as you're told, Jo Pitts, or ye'll
live to rue the day ye came back!" Buck Hogan
hollered, shoving Sara.

❧❧❧

With a whoop and a holler, Jo pushed Hetty overboard.
The poor woman sank, then rose sputtering in shock
as Jo rowed merrily away.

"Sara is our niece," said Hetty.

The others listened, all ears, waiting for a pearl of wisdom. Hetty hesitated, looking back at the outhouse, which was shaking and creaking from all the pounding. With a heavy heart, she turned back to the circle.

"We owe it to Ruth's memory to keep this private...and to treat the child nicely."

Janet and Olivia straightened up. "Nicely?" they said, astonished.

"I've made up my mind," announced Hetty. "We have to let her out of there."

Olivia opened her mouth to object but Hetty silenced her.

"We have no choice. From now on, we will handle Sara Stanley by...humoring her."

"But, Hetty!" gasped Olivia. "What if it doesn't work?"

"I am still the head of this family," said Hetty, drawing herself up with as much dignity as she could muster while her niece screamed from the outhouse. "What I say goes. Sara is our dear sister's daughter and we have an obligation, at the very least, to be kind. From now on, we will humor her."

"Watch out, Hetty!" screamed Olivia.

Too late. With a horrible crash the entire outhouse exploded, the walls tumbling and smashing on top of Hetty. Jo Pitts leapt out, screaming like a wild animal, and tore across the fields to freedom.

"Here we go again," muttered Olivia, hanging on to her hat, hiking up her skirts and racing after Jo Pitts with more determination than ever. A split second later, Janet was racing behind Olivia, hollering at the top of her lungs.

Behind all of them, Hetty King lay sprawled on the ground, surrounded by the debris of the outhouse. Dazed and defeated, with tears brimming in her eyes, she struggled to her knees and watched as Janet and Olivia chased the young girl across the meadows.

"Dear Lord," she murmured, her hands clasped in earnest prayer, "why is this happening? Help me to understand! Give us back our little Sara!"

Chapter Eleven

The rain struck with a fury, and water poured in torrents through the gutters. In the harbor, tall ships shuddered and swayed as the wind gusted. All night long the wind howled and the rain came down in gray, dismal sheets.

On the slippery deck of a cargo ship, Abe Pike lifted a heavy trapdoor and shoved two passengers into the hold.

"That's where ye'll stay," he growled, "till we're safe an' snug in Kingston harbor."

With that he locked the trapdoor with its key and turned his scarred face to the relentless storm. It would be the wee hours of the morning before the torrential rains ran their course. No point setting sail till then. Through the mist, he could just make out the twinkling lights of the tavern. Abe was torn. With his captives locked tight below deck, surely there was time enough to warm his insides with a glass or two of grog? He shivered and kicked the trapdoor for good measure. No point getting soaked, not for the sake of his worthless son and that traitor, Jo Pitts. He turned up the collar of his jacket and disembarked, heading quickly for the lights of the tavern.

Below, in the dark hold packed with wooden crates, Sara and Gus heard the sound of Abe's footsteps crossing the deck.

Gus turned sorrowfully to Sara. "I got us into a fine mess this time, Sara."

"I still don't understand!" whispered Sara, who was frightened and confused by this turn of events.

"I had to get you away from the lot of them, from Buck and his pack o' thieves. I had to pretend I was on their side," he explained. "The one thing I didn't count on was Abe leavin' so soon for Jamaica!"

"Jamaica!"

"I had to make up a tale about Captain Crane. Jamaica was the first place that popped into my skull!" He looked around in dismay. "An' here we be, caught like rats in a trap, not a hope of escape, all on accounta they think you're Jo Pitts."

"I know." Sara felt sick at the thought of telling Gus her own part in this disaster. "Please don't be mad at me, Gus. I left Jo Pitts back in Avonlea. It was just a game. Jo Pitts took my place for a while so I could have a holiday from Aunt Hetty."

Gus groaned and hit his head with his hand. "You never tol' me that part of it! I never woulda let ya come with me if I knew! That was real stupid, Sara, *real* stupid."

"I know," said Sara remorsefully, wishing with all her heart that she could shrivel up and blow away in the storm. She had been selfish and foolish, and what had she gained? Nothing. Not only had she put herself in danger, but now Gus Pike was at risk too—Gus, who was her dearest friend in the world!

Gus glanced upward. "Sara, look." He pointed to a small porthole above their heads. "It's the only chance you've got. Climb on those crates and get out. Quick, before Abe comes back."

"I'm not going without you!" exclaimed Sara.

"Oh yes you are. I can't squeeze through that hole, but you can. Do as I say. Go!" His eyes burned fiercely. *"Go! There's no time to lose."*

Sara's breath froze in her lungs. She knew Gus was right. Perhaps if she escaped she could run for help.

Gus nodded as if reading her thoughts. Without a word, she scaled the crates and shoved the porthole open. She took one look back at him, frightened she might never see him again. Then she twisted through the narrow opening and dropped with a thud on the deck.

Alone in the dark hold, Gus could hear the sound of her footsteps running along the deck overhead. Then an awful silence. Holding his breath, he prayed Abe Pike hadn't spotted her! If she used her head she could leap overboard and...

Then suddenly, directly above him, he heard the key in the lock and the creak of the trapdoor being lifted. Gus groaned. Abe! He'd caught her! Now they were done for.

But instead it was Sara's face peering down into the dark, her voice piping excitedly, "Hurry, Gus...he left the key in the lock!"

Swiftly he leapt the stairs two at a time and

bounded onto the deck. The trapdoor clanged shut behind him. He grabbed Sara's hand.

"Good work!" he whispered. "Let's run for it!"

Chapter Twelve

"Oh, allow me, Sara dear," Hetty murmured sweetly, slathering gobs of butter on a huge stack of pancakes. She had barely finished buttering and pouring maple syrup when Jo Pitts speared the entire stack and wolfed them down, wiping her mouth with the back of her hand and, with her mouth still full, demanding more.

Hetty hastily filled up the empty plate. "Would you like me to butter them for you?"

"Quit pesterin' me, will ya?" snarled Jo Pitts.

Hetty leapt back in alarm, fearful of annoying her young charge. Sara looked dreadful, her hair wild and unkempt, her face smeared with dirt and her good blue dress stained and torn in several places. Hetty resolved not to comment. Respectfully, she watched Jo shovel in the rest of the stack. Then, when the last syrup-soaked morsel had disappeared, Hetty wrung her hands nervously and approached the table once again.

"Sara," she asked with great trepidation, "do you think, after you finish your breakfast...I'm not rushing you, mind you, take as long as you wish...but I wondered if perhaps you might like to tidy up your room?"

"Nope."

Hetty sucked in her breath. "Fine, fine, that's absolutely fine, don't get upset, dear." She peered anxiously at Jo. "You don't have to do *anything*, dear. You can just sit and twiddle your thumbs, if that's what you desire."

Jo looked up at her thoughtfully. Yes, she had to admit, the eats were the best—plentiful, and delicious, too—better than any grub Jo had tasted in her years of scavenging from garbage cans on the mainland. Buck and Rat and the gang never had it so good. And the service! Nothing to complain about there, either! Hetty King was waiting on her hand and foot, cooking, cleaning, ironing clothes and washing linens and catering to every wild whim that popped into Jo's head. Still, something was wrong. A simple fact was nagging at the edge of Jo's crafty little brain: *time was running out.*

Jo forced herself to remember why she had come to Avonlea in the first place. It wasn't to sit around eating pancakes. She'd had a purpose back then, a plan. She'd intended to pick the town clean of its riches, escape in the dead of night and flee to the next unsuspecting village. There she would repeat the performance, collect enough loot and add it to her stash. Eventually, when she had accumulated enough treasure, she could steal back to the mainland and cash it all in! Then she would show Buck Hogan and his gang of hooligans just who was king of the heap. Then *she* could call the shots with nobody else butting in, not even that vicious Abe Pike who had all of them under his thumb!

Jo was looking for a hideaway. She was sick and tired of dodging shadows in the night, running from town to town one step ahead of the law. She was weary of looking over her shoulder, scared to stop and rest her bones, lest some constable nose around and start asking questions. Maybe she'd got a bit sidetracked, but, truth be told, Sara's little invite had come along in the nick of time. Jo Pitts fancied a vacation, same as Sara did, maybe more! And if trading places was the answer to Sara's prayers, for Jo Pitts it was a dream come true!

At first Jo relished the danger, the challenge. Could she hoodwink Hetty King, or would she be caught red-handed and thrown out on her ear? Then, little by little, she had stopped worrying. Everyone, Hetty included, had accepted her as Sara. One sunny day began to melt into another, and Jo had settled into Rose Cottage as if she belonged there. Oh, she still loved outwitting Hetty at every turn, making the old sourpuss feel sorry for her and do her bidding at the snap of a finger. But something unexpected had happened, something Jo hadn't counted on.

She began to *like* being Sara.

She liked waking up in a pretty room on soft pillows and linens that smelled fresh and sweet as the roses that bloomed outside her window. She liked the delicious pies and cakes Hetty seemed to conjure up at will. She even liked the attention from that pack of sugar-sweet relatives, Olivia and Janet and Jasper and Alec, the lot of them forever yammering away at her: *Are you well, Sara? Are you happy? Are you feeling better, dear?* Why, she'd never felt better in her life—any lamebrained fool could see that! Mind you, Felix King was a bit of a nuisance, worrying and fretting about nothing, but he was a cupcake compared to Buck Hogan and Rat and Mole.

No, all things considered, life wasn't half bad around here. Lately, she had even taken to daydreaming. She imagined what it would like staying in Avonlea forever, living in luxury in Rose Cottage, with Hetty King as her cook and personal servant.

That, thought Jo ruefully, must never happen. She could not allow herself to be lulled into contentment, because that would be changing the rules of the game. This was supposed to be a vacation, but vacations had to end. Besides, something was nagging at her and it wasn't Hetty.

Jo Pitts was discovering a truth about herself. All play and no work gave her the willies.

She had come to Avonlea, not for a holiday, but to complete a task. A simple task, really, one she had sorely neglected of late: to pluck Rose Cottage clean of its goodies.

And what goodies they were! Silver and china, gold pins and watches! They would bring a fortune on the mainland. If she didn't take what she'd come for in the first place, if she didn't act quickly...it might be too late! A terrible thought had been creeping into her mind as she drifted off to sleep at night. What if Sara Stanley took it into her head to cut her vacation short? A shiver ran up Jo's spine. Sara could traipse through that front door, breeze into the kitchen, smile that smile of hers and reclaim her rightful place without a care in the world for Jo! Yes sirree, thought Jo, Sara's return would throw a monkey wrench into everything.

Jo's brow furrowed, a plan brewing. No more laziness, no more snuggling down under feather quilts smelling the roses and pretending she was a little princess. She had to collect her wits, act quickly, or the jig would be up.

Idly, she twirled her knife and looked up at

Hetty, who was wiping crumbs off the kitchen table. "Hey, you!" Jo said sharply.

Hetty looked up with trepidation. Jo flashed her a winning smile. "I was just thinkin', it's a real nice day. How's about a picnic, ya old bag?"

Old bag? Blood rushed to Hetty's head. In the old days she would have cheerfully tanned a child's bottom for indulging in such indelicate, disrespectful language. But not now. Now she restrained herself.

"A picnic?" she murmured, all sweetness and light. "Of course. Yes. Charming. Who shall we invite? Felix and Felicity?"

"Nope," replied Jo Pitts. "Just me...an' you."

Sheer delight caused Hetty to flush from her throat to her cheeks. Wonder of wonders! Sara wanted to go on a picnic, just the two of them? Hetty was thrilled. This was *progress!*

"Isn't that a lovely idea, dear!" she replied, leaning over and fondly patting the top of Jo's blond head. "I do believe you are on the mend, child. I'll make some sandwiches and lemonade as quickly as I can!"

Hetty bustled about the kitchen filling the picnic hamper in preparation for a wonderful sun-filled afternoon. Behind her back, Jo Pitts stuck the knife into the table and carved a miniature skull and crossbones, which she hastily covered up with the cream pitcher when Hetty turned to beam at her.

Sunlight broke like a thousand glittering diamonds on the calm waters as Jo Pitts rowed the little craft across the lake. Hetty King sat primly under her blue umbrella, the picnic hamper safely ensconced on her lap. Every now and then, she dipped her hand into the water and plucked a lily pad.

"Have you ever seen anything so beautiful, Sara?" she crooned, her heart bursting with happiness at the sight of Sara's face tilted to the sun, innocent and pale, like this lily she held in her hands.

"There's the island," said Jo. "We're almost there."

"Lovely," purred Hetty, settling back and enjoying the gentle sway of the little boat as it sliced through the water. She could hardly wait to tell Janet and Olivia what a perfectly wonderful day she was having. Smiling smugly to herself, she savored the moment when she would point out the success of her theory. Specialists and nerve tonic indeed! Kindness had done the trick, and here was the proof, the two of them on their way to a picnic, Sara rowing the boat as full of vim and vigor as anyone could wish.

Jo peered slyly at Hetty. So far so good. The ol' bat didn't suspect a thing. In fact, she seemed to be enjoying herself. Jo could hardly suppress a chortle of glee. Before this trip was over, Hetty King would get the surprise of her life. Still, thought Jo, rowing was awful hard work. Her arms were sore from the effort. And it was getting hot, what with the sun broiling down on the little tub of a boat. Jo wiped perspiration from her brow. All this exercise was making her grumpy, and hungry as a bear. She eyed the picnic hamper, thinking of the delectable goodies inside. Too bad they would go to waste. Licking her lips, for the briefest of moments she considered a pause in her plans, stopping to munch on one of those tasty chicken sandwiches right this very minute. Then, just as quickly, her resolve hardened. She must not think about chicken. She must think of the worst possible event...the surprise return of Sara Stanley. She must concentrate solely on the goal, the treasures waiting at Rose Cottage.

Hetty shaded her eyes from the sun and squinted back to see the shoreline of the little island. With a start, she realized Sara was rowing off course.

"Sara dear," she said with a frown, "don't get out of sorts, but I suspect you're rowing in the wrong direction. The island is the other way."

"No I ain't," replied Jo, rowing even more vigorously, "'cuz we ain't goin' to no island. We're goin' to China."

Hetty gasped. China? Good Lord...here she thought Sara was on her way to recovery and she was more addled than ever! Hetty chose her words carefully.

"Sara, I don't think it's a good idea to go to China."

"Why not?" snickered Jo.

"Because—" and now Hetty bit her lip nervously before continuing—"because, you see, dear, China isn't exactly where I thought we were going."

"Too bad," growled Jo. "Ain't ya havin' a good time no more?"

"I'm having a *wonderful* time!" was Hetty's hasty reply. "But perhaps you might want to let me row for a bit?"

"Oh sure," said Jo, leaping to her feet, causing the craft to sway tipsily. "Trade ya places."

"*Be careful!*" cried Hetty. "One mustn't stand up in a boat...one must creep carefully...like so." With that, she gingerly got down on all fours and crawled towards Jo, who grinned devilishly and began to jump up and down, rocking the boat until it lurched precariously from side to side. Hetty clutched at the gunwales. "No! No! Don't do that!" she screamed, suddenly forgetting her own warning and standing up to stop Jo. "We're going to have an accident!"

Too late. With a whoop and a holler, Jo shoved Hetty overboard. The poor woman sank, then rose sputtering in shock as Jo rowed merrily away, chuckling at the sight of Hetty dog-paddling furiously to keep afloat.

"Sara Stanley! You come back here this

instant!" screamed Hetty, spitting out a mouth-
ful of water and gasping for air. "I can't swim!"

"What a whopper," muttered Jo to herself.
Hetty King had lived near water all her life.
Certainly she knew how to swim!

"Bye-bye, ya old bat," yelled Jo Pitts,
rowing towards land, blithely ignoring Hetty's
plea for help.

Jo Pitts dashed across the meadow towards
Rose Cottage, her fiendish little mind racing a
mile a minute. If she could get into Rose Cottage before anyone noticed Hetty was missing,
she could strip the place clean in a flash...pro-
viding none of those miserable Kings stuck
their big fat noses into her business.

"Hey! Wait up, Jo!"

She stopped dead in her tracks. Speak of
the devil, there was Felix King running
towards her. Rotten luck! Now she'd have to
waste time chit-chatting with the dumpy little
bird-brain.

"I've been looking all over for you!" panted
Felix, stopping to catch his breath. "Mother told
us they locked you in the outhouse yesterday!"

"Yeah. Buncha ol' hags, the lot of 'em," muttered Jo, hurrying towards Rose Cottage.

"Listen, stop for a minute," said Felix.

"Can't. I got stuff to do."

"I just want to talk to you. Things have gone too far. You've got everyone thinking Sara's crazy and Aunt Hetty's in a real tizzy about it!"

"Forget about *her*."

"What do you mean?" asked Felix.

"Oh, nothin'," Jo tossed off nonchalantly. "I just left the ol' bat in the middle of the lake."

"YOU WHAT?" cried Felix, backing away from her in horror. He stood there stunned for a moment, then turned tail and ran towards the King farm.

Jo cackled to herself. Just what she'd planned! If she hurried, she could rob Rose Cottage of all its treasures and be long gone before Felix blabbed to his parents, who naturally wouldn't believe him and would waste all sorts of valuable time while they dithered around and finally decided to investigate. Jo Pitts was certainly glad she'd stumbled across these ignorant yokels. Compared with some folks, the Kings were pushovers.

Felix tore into the kitchen, yelling at the top of his lungs. "She *drowned* her, she *drowned* her! Come QUICK!"

Janet, who was standing at the counter chopping vegetables for soup, turned and looked at her son. "Who drowned whom, Felix?" she asked calmly, accustomed to outbursts of various sorts from her excitable offspring. "I do wish you'd wash your face. You look as though you've run a mile. Whatever is wrong?"

"I just *told* you, Mother!" cried Felix, "It's Sara! I don't know how to explain this—don't get mad at me, but she isn't Sara." There. It was out. He looked desperately at his mother. Janet, however, merely returned to chopping her vegetables.

"I know, dear," she said sympathetically. "Sara hasn't been herself lately."

"No, no!" exclaimed Felix. "That's not what I meant! She says...Sara says...I mean, she just said she went and drowned Aunt Hetty!"

This time Janet stopped chopping. "What?"

"Sara drowned Aunt Hetty!" cried Felix.

"Good Lord!" Janet went chalk white.

"We have to find the body!" choked Felix. "Hurry!"

"The body...!" Horrified, Janet threw her apron aside, grabbed Felix by the hand and went tearing wildly out the door in search of Hetty King.

Chapter Thirteen

A wagonload of squawking chickens rumbled along the red dirt road, heading for Avonlea. The driver, a grizzled old farmer taking his chickens to market, reined in his ancient sway-backed horse and called out to a couple of dusty passengers perched on top of a crate. "There ye be, folks. You're home."

Sara and Gus jumped off the back of the wagon. "Thank you, sir," Sara called out. "I wish I could pay you but we haven't a penny between us!"

The old man, who was grateful for any shred of human conversation on the lonely road from town to town, brushed aside Sara's offer of payment with a wave of his hand. "Think

nothin' of it. I was headed this way anyhow."
He chucked the horse on and the wagon
lurched ahead with its squawking cargo.

Sara looked around her. Ahead lay the
sunny meadows filled with nodding wildflow-
ers and tall, billowing grasses. She breathed
deeply, filling her lungs with the fragrant air,
tinged with a faint hint of the sea.

"I never thought I'd see Avonlea again,"
she said rapturously. "I love every dear, sweet
inch of it."

Gus, who never in his wildest dreams
thought he'd find a place to call home,
couldn't help smiling in agreement. He was
more than grateful to be back in the peace and
tranquility of this quaint little town; in fact, he
was almost tempted to kneel and kiss the
rough red dirt under his feet. Instead, he
looked sternly down at Sara.

"I hope this taught ya a lesson, Sara Stanley."

"Oh it did!" breathed Sara, running ahead
of him in her eagerness to see Rose Cottage.
"Come home with me, Gus. Help me explain
all of this to Aunt Hetty! If you're there, I just
know she'll understand."

"No ya don't," said Gus. "I ain't bailin' ya outta this mess, so don't shift the blame onto me. After leavin' her with a pickpocket in your place, I think ya better face your aunt Hetty yourself."

Sara looked chagrined. Gus was right. It was up to her to face the fireworks alone. And fireworks it would be, for Aunt Hetty would be up in arms when she heard how Sara's little "lark" had turned into a nightmare, complete with hoodlums and kidnapping and all sorts of dark and nameless terrors.

Gus took pity on her. "It won't be so bad, Sara. The truth only hurts in the tellin'. It was me what dragged ya into the mess, what with Abe Pike and all. You an' me, I guess we were both kinda stupid!"

"Thanks for saying so, Gus Pike. You're a dear, true friend and I'll never forget it!" said Sara passionately. "But this whole thing was more my fault than yours. I was dead wrong to leave home." Then she looked up at him earnestly. "But I'm not wrong about coming back! I'm ready to own up to my mistakes. So wish me luck!" With that, she took off across the meadows, turning to wave just once, heading for home.

Gus watched her run. He wished her luck, that he did. Sara was brave, a sight braver than he would be in her shoes. She hadn't bawled once all the time they were in danger, the way most girls would've. And, if the tables were turned, he wasn't sure *he* could face up to Hetty King's temper with half so much courage.

Chapter Fourteen

A huge burlap sack was spread out on the parlor floor in Rose Cottage, and as fast as she could, Jo Pitts was stuffing it with booty. Into the sack went the silver cream and sugar bowl, the teapot and tongs and the tray from Grandfather King's beautiful tea service.

Swiftly she looked around. What had she forgotten? Her eyes lit on the chased-silver water pitcher! That would bring a pretty penny in the thieves' market! She snatched it off the mahogany table, scraping the table's fine finish and knocking over the crystal lamp, which smashed to smithereens.

"Drat it!" she muttered.

Kicking the shards aside, she dumped out the drawers of the sideboard and scooped up a handful of pearl-handled fish forks, biting the tines to make sure they were really silver. She chuckled with delight! This was like taking candy from a baby! With a haul like this, she'd show that greedy Buck Hogan who was boss. Rat and Mole and the others would look at her with new eyes. They wouldn't work for Abe Pike any more. No doubt about it. If she played her cards right, she'd be running the show, and the whole slimy gang of pickpockets on the mainland would be under her command.

A quick glance at the ticking clock told her she had precious little time to waste. A few minutes to strip the china cabinet of its silver doodads, a fast rifling of the old bat's chifforobe to find the gold watch she sometimes left pinned to a blouse, and she'd have everything worth stealing from this dump of a place they called Rose Cottage! She giggled with glee. When she was finished plucking it bare, they'd call it Rose Garbage Can!

Chapter Fifteen

Terror-stricken, Janet and Felix raced helter-skelter towards the seashore, screaming Hetty's name. Suddenly they stopped dead in their tracks.

"No...!" whispered Janet, shading her eyes and staring straight ahead. "I can't believe it! It can't be... "

Crawling up the beach on all fours was a soaking-wet creature, barefoot and bedraggled... and every few moments the creature paused and moaned as though half dead.

"Oh my heavens!" gasped Janet. "It's Hetty!"

Janet reached Hetty just as she struggled to her knees and then fell again.

"Is she alive?" cried Felix.

"Speak to me!" demanded Janet. "Please, Hetty, I beg of you, say something!"

"Swam..." moaned Hetty, flailing weakly at thin air. "Where is she...? Want to throttle her—"

she struggled with all her might to finish the thought "—have her committed...have myself committed..." With that, she wavered and collapsed.

In a panic, Janet tried to pull her up. "Take her feet, Felix," she ordered. "I'll take her hands!"

They hoisted the waterlogged Hetty up the beach, slipping and sliding and stumbling the entire way. They managed to drag her up a steep incline and down a gully. Then, staggering towards the road, they headed back to Rose Cottage. Hetty was out cold, and thus mercifully oblivious to the indignity of having her skirt riding up over her bare ankles.

Jo Pitts slithered out the parlor window with her sack of booty in the nick of time, for mere moments later an excited Sara Stanley came racing through the gate and up to the front door.

Her heart beating wildly, Sara nervously smoothed her hair and dusted off her dress. With a deep breath, she opened the door.

"Aunt Hetty!" she cried out. "I'm home!"

Dead silence.

"Aunt Hetty...?"

Still no answer. Puzzled, Sara ran into the kitchen. She stifled a cry. Every drawer was pulled out and the contents dumped hither and thither. Sara dashed into the parlor and, to her horror, found it a shambles as well—the crystal lamp smashed, pictures awry, chairs overturned, once-gleaming tabletops now bereft of treasures. Thoroughly shaken, she dashed upstairs, frightened for Aunt Hetty's safety, racing from room to room and finding disaster everywhere she turned. But her aunt was nowhere to be found.

Suddenly she heard the front door open. Flying downstairs again, she cried out, "Oh Aunt Hetty..." Then she fell silent. Aunt Janet and Felix were dragging Hetty inside. By now she had regained consciousness but could barely stand.

"Aunt Hetty...what happened?" exclaimed Sara, flinging her arms around Hetty's neck.

"Don't touch me!" screamed Hetty, leaping back and pulling Janet between Sara and herself, as though she had just seen Satan in the flesh.

Sara stared from one to the other, bewildered.

"Now Sara..." cautioned Janet, guarding Hetty with one hand and fending off Sara with another. Fearful of setting off one of Sara's dreadful temper tantrums, she whispered quickly to Felix, "Be careful, don't get her worked up! She could be dangerous." Then, turning to Sara, she murmured in the most soothing tones she could muster, considering the circumstances, "Sara! How are you, dear?"

"I'm fine, Aunt Janet! And I'm so happy to see all of you!" Sara smiled from ear to ear, but she was crestfallen when she received no smile in return. She knew her homecoming wouldn't be easy, but in her heart of hearts she had hoped for some warmth and affection, some sign of forgiveness.

"We...uh...stumbled across Aunt Hetty dripping wet, Sara. Can you imagine such a thing?" Aunt Janet's voice oozed sweetness, but to Sara the smile seemed forced. "You don't suppose she went swimming, do you?" continued Janet, her voice trembling.

Sara looked at her blankly. Why was Aunt Janet asking such ridiculous questions? Why were they all staring at her so suspiciously? And why was Aunt Hetty shivering and hiding behind Janet's skirts?

"Aunt Hetty's never gone swimming in her entire life. You know that very well! Please tell me what's wrong, Aunt Janet! Poor Aunt Hetty! Why are you soaking wet? And what on earth happened to the house?"

"What about the house?" blurted Aunt Janet.

Sara gestured around her. "It looks like someone ransacked it!"

Now it was their turn to be shocked. Seeing for the first time the state of havoc, Janet gasped, and her hand flew to her heart as though she might faint. Hetty was speechless.

Flabbergasted, Felix looked at Sara, then at the mess, then back at Sara, unsure what to believe. "Sara," he whispered tentatively, "is that *you*?"

"Of course it's me, silly!" Sara whispered back. "I just returned with Gus Pike."

"Gracious Providence!" cried Janet as she inspected the topsy-turvy parlor. "This place looks like a hurricane's been through!"

"Dear Aunt Hetty," murmured Sara, "let me get you a blanket. Your lips are turning blue!"

"NO! NO!" shrieked Hetty. "Don't let her near me. She's up to something!"

"Hetty King, *pipe down!*" cried Janet, "or I'm going to have a conniption fit myself! The silver's gone! All of Grandfather King's beautiful silver, disappeared!"

"Please, won't someone tell me what's going on?" pleaded Sara.

"Now, now, dear, don't you start!" trilled Janet, her nerves at the breaking point as she moved slowly and carefully towards Sara. "Aunt Hetty is upset, you're upset, we're all upset, so let's just stand here calmly and quietly while I decide what to do." Her voice quavered and her hands were shaking so violently that Sara reached out to calm her. "NO!" Janet screamed.

Sara froze. Something awful had happened to her family during her absence and she was determined to get to the bottom of it! "Aunt Janet, I'm afraid there's been a terrible misunderstanding."

"There has NOT been a misunderstanding!" hollered Aunt Hetty. "Look at me! Look at my house!"

"But I can explain everything," said Sara. "You see, it was just a silly lark...!"

Janet's eyes rolled. A lark? The poor thing actually thought drowning Hetty was a lark? "I am loath to say this, Sara Stanley," she said very, very cautiously, "and don't take it the wrong way, dearest heart, but"—and now her voice fell to a bare whisper—"you have lost your mind. And you're making everyone else lose theirs!"

"Oh no, Aunt Janet, you're wrong," replied Sara earnestly. Her heart sank. How could Aunt Janet accuse her of such terrible things? Was it possible they really thought she was to blame for the theft of the family silver? She hadn't meant to hurt anyone, and now the whole family was in an uproar. How would she ever make them all understand!

Chapter Sixteen

A small, blond figure hauling a heavy burlap sack darted out of a stand of dark firs, made a dash through the cherry orchard, then crept furtively up the slopes past the lighthouse. "Dratted sunlight," Jo Pitts muttered under her breath, pausing to catch her breath and readjust the weight of the heavy sack. She knew she should hide until dark, but the temptation to be on her way was too great, for now that she had plucked Avonlea clean, she was anxious to find greener pastures.

Still, just to be on the safe side, she ducked her head and ran as fast as she could with her awkward baggage. Just a few yards more and she would be safely on the red dirt road leading out of Avonlea, far from prying eyes.

The hand that clutched her shoulder caught her totally off guard.

"Sara?" said a firm voice.

Jo Pitts gulped. There was Gus Pike. Where had he come from? Sprung out of the blue like a ghost? She managed a half smile and brushed a stray curl from her eyes.

"I thought you was headin' home, Sara," said Gus. He thumped the burlap sack. "Hey. What's this?"

"Oh...nothin'," muttered Jo, wishing he would go back where he came from and let her be on her way. "Just some...presents...for Aunt Hetty."

Gus eyed her carefully. "Presents?"

"Yeah, presents. Dintcha hear me the first time?" said Jo arrogantly.

"I heard ya," replied Gus. "Those ain't presents. An' you ain't Sara Stanley."

For the briefest possible moment, Jo considered buying time by outmaneuvering him. One look into those dark, earnest eyes and she knew it was useless trying to out-fox, out-do or out-talk the likes of Gus Pike. Instead she kicked him square in the shin and bolted like a rabbit down the slopes.

Gus howled and grasped his shin, then raced after her, making a swift grab for the burlap sack. The contents spilled to the ground. "I'll be a monkey's uncle!" he gasped as silver urns and candlesticks tumbled across the grass.

Jo was scrambling towards the road when Gus made a flying leap and nabbed her by the ankles. They both went sprawling, but Gus, being the stronger of the two, quickly pinned her to the ground.

"You'll pay for this, Gus Pike!" she screamed, trying to bite his hand.

"Think ya got that wrong," said Gus. She was still kicking and screaming when he threw her over his shoulder like a bag of flour. With his free hand, he stuffed the booty back into the sack and slowly hauled the struggling thief and her hard-won loot along the red dirt road, back to the scene of the crime.

Sara was not faring well. Janet and Olivia sat on the sofa, on either side of Hetty, with the strangest expressions on their faces. What was worse, Hetty was cowering between them, shivering and terrified, shrinking back from Sara as though she were a she-devil instead of a contrite little girl come home to repent. Sara's heart sank.

Gus had warned her. And she herself had worried that her return might be complicated, but she had never envisioned a reception as chilly as this. What on earth had gone wrong?

"But don't you see?" pleaded Sara. "You thought she was me!"

Janet, Olivia and Hetty exchanged skeptical glances. They shifted uncomfortably on the sofa where they perched like three suspicious crows, listening to Sara's explanation. They looked at her dumfounded. It certainly looked like Sara. It even sounded like Sara. But...*was it Sara?* She sat primly, hands folded, on Sara's favorite chair, the needlepoint Queen Anne, the one Blair Stanley had given Ruth upon their engagement.

"Would you repeat that, dear, the part about you thinking that she was you?" asked Aunt Olivia, her brow wrinkling. "Or was it she thinking you were her? I'm afraid I don't understand!"

"Neither do I," said Janet. "Who thought who was you?"

"The girl who looked like me," replied Sara impatiently.

"And who might that be?" was Olivia's wary response.

"Jo Pitts!" cried Sara, jumping up from her chair. "That's what I've been trying to tell you. She was pretending to be me, only she didn't tell me who she really was."

Another swift exchange of looks. "I see," said Olivia, not seeing at all. "If you'll sit still, Sara, perhaps we can—"

"Shhh!" interjected Janet. "Don't get her all nervous, Olivia. Lord knows what she'll do!"

"But that's the point!" insisted Sara. "I'm not nervous. Anyone would get confused if they thought I was someone else. But I'm not! And I wasn't! I wasn't even here, and what's even stranger is that everyone *there* thought I was someone else too!"

A mystified silence fell as Janet and Olivia's eyes rolled towards Hetty, who sat white-faced and thin-lipped.

"I told you we should get a specialist down here!" hissed Janet. "They know what to do with these cases!"

"If you'd let me finish, Aunt Janet, I'd

explain it all!" cried Sara, getting thoroughly exasperated. "You see, the other girl—"

"We know that, dear," said Olivia. "They're both you."

"No, no!" exclaimed Sara. "You just *think* they're both me, but they're not! The awful part is she's very dangerous, and she never told me, so no wonder you're upset!"

"*Make her stop!*" shrieked Hetty, clapping her hands over her ears. "I can't stand listening to another word!" She seized a pillow and held it over her head. Olivia and Janet jumped up, all in a dither, and in the midst of this bedlam the door burst open.

Gus Pike entered the room, hauling a bulging burlap sack in one hand and a squirming, defiant Jo Pitts in the other.

Hetty turned chalk white. "That's it!" she sobbed, collapsing into a heap on the sofa. "Now I see two of them! Somebody help me! It's a nightmare!"

"It ain't no nightmare, Miss King," said Gus, dumping the contents of the sack on the parlor rug.

Hetty and the others stared in horror as the

gleaming pieces of Grandfather King's sterling silver tea service appeared before their eyes.

"Now just one minute!" demanded Janet, collecting her wits. "What is going on here?" She turned on Sara. "Who are you?"

"I'm me, Aunt Janet."

Janet paused, discombobulated. She whirled around and waggled her finger under Jo Pitts's nose. "And who are *you*?" she demanded.

Jo pursed her lips. "I ain't talkin' to none o' you ol' bats."

"That's Jo Pitts," said Gus matter-of-factly.

"Jo Pitts?" chorused Hetty and Olivia and Janet.

"That's what I've been trying to tell you!" said Sara.

"Oh Lord help us," cried Janet.

Hetty, Janet and Olivia stared at the two blond girls. They could barely tell one from the other.

"Mother, you'd better sit down." Felix took his mother's arm and plunked her in a chair before she keeled over from shock.

"You see, Felix and I met her one day," explained Sara.

"And she was wearing the dress, the one that Sara bought and Aunt Hetty gave away," chimed in Felix.

"I never stole it!" hollered Jo Pitts. "I got it from the poor box, an' that' ain't stealin', no matter how ya slice it!"

Janet turned abruptly on Felix. "And just what part did you play in all of this, young man?"

Felix reddened, casting a quick glance at Sara for support.

"It was all my idea, Aunt Janet," Sara said.

"I only went along with it at first to fool Felicity," mumbled Felix, grateful to Sara for taking the brunt of the blame but feeling a little guilty all the same.

"And when we had so much fun tricking Felicity," continued Sara, "that's when we thought it might be a lark if Jo and I changed places for a few days."

"*Changed places!*" exclaimed Aunt Hetty, almost relieved to hear the truth. "So that's what happened!" Still shivering, she turned towards Sara and said weakly, "You don't know the pain you've caused me."

"Oh Aunt Hetty, I do! I know it was wrong, I know it now with all my heart!" Sara was fighting hard to hold back tears. "And I'd never ever do it again, but I was so angry and fed up with you!"

"Fed up with me?" was Hetty's astounded reply. "How could you say such a terrible thing! Why, I've never done a thing that wasn't for your own good!"

"But you were so strict with me all the time, and I didn't know what else to do."

"What else to *do*?" cried Hetty. "Why, if you'd had a grain of common sense—"

"I think," said Olivia, placing a hand on Hetty's arm, "that everyone concerned made errors in...judgment, and we're about to make another one if we don't get you out of those soaking-wet clothes and bundled into something nice and warm!"

"Hetty dear," said Janet, helping Hetty to her feet and taking her arm, "why don't you come upstairs with me?"

Hetty shook free of Janet's arm. "I'm not an invalid, Janet King! I can manage myself!" Proudly, she stumbled to the stairs, where she faltered and had to catch herself against the wall for support. Janet hurried to her side and assisted her sister-in-law up the stairs.

"Guess I'm leaving," announced Jo loftily. She scooted for the door, but Gus Pike and Olivia hauled her back.

"You sit down and do as you're told!" cried Olivia, pulling out a chair.

Jo Pitts refused the offer. "I ain't sittin' with the likes o' you," she muttered, and she stood in the corner with her arms folded defiantly. Gus declined a chair as well, and instead stood guard at the kitchen door in case Jo took it into her head to bolt again.

Olivia bustled about the kitchen heating the kettle and slicing bread for sandwiches. She sighed wearily. "In situations like this," she said, surveying the motley crew assembled, "I suppose what is called for is a nice hot cup of tea."

Chapter Seventeen

Luckily, Hetty King's larder was well stocked with provisions—cold chicken, cheeses and an assortment of pickles, jams and cakes. The hearty offering was just what the doctor ordered, for everyone was famished. Sara and Gus relished each and every morsel, declaring the crusty sandwiches food fit for the gods.

Jo Pitts, however, refused to comment, insisting instead on crouching on the floor in the corner of the kitchen, sullenly munching on buttery crusts and licking her fingers in silence. From this vantage point, she pretended a total lack of interest in the table talk, but sly glances in Sara's direction indicated that she was soaking up every word as Sara told the horrifying tale of Abe Pike and The Black Parrot, of Buck and Rat and Mole and the rest of the gang of thieves and pickpockets. As Sara spoke, Jo knew that her dream of a triumphant return to the gang was just that...a foolish dream. How the boys would sneer if they could see her now, cornered like a rat in a trap, with nothing to show for her efforts but a crust of bread. Jo stole a look at Hetty, who listened aghast to Sara's tale, and groaned. Lord knew what the ol' bat would do in revenge!

Hetty, however, was too appalled to think

04   ROAD TO AVONLEA

of revenge. She huddled under a thick quilt, an
ice pack on her aching head and her feet soaking in a pail of steaming hot water. She was
just tucking into her third slice of plum cake
when Janet offered her another.

"No thank you," she muttered, waving the
plum cake aside with a martyred sigh. "Rat...
Mole...thieves and pickpockets. It's enough to
make a person lose her appetite."

"Oh nonsense. Have another," insisted
Janet. "After what you've been through, Hetty
King, you have to keep up your strength."

"You're right," agreed Hetty, digging with
relish into yet another moist slice of plum cake.

"I can't imagine how you kept your wits
about you in the face of such danger, Sara!"
said Olivia, filled with a mixture of admiration
and horror. "My head is absolutely bursting!"

Sara rose from her chair and stood beside
Hetty. Gently, she leaned over and kissed
Hetty on the cheek. "What kept me going was
you, Aunt Hetty," she said softly.

"Me? I thought it was me you were running
away from," said Hetty, both delighted and
embarrassed by the tender kiss.

"I'm truly sorry I caused so much trouble," whispered Sara.

"Well, it's over and done with," said Hetty, briskly patting Sara's hand. "I missed the old Sara, I can tell you!" She turned gratefully to Gus. "Thank you for bringing her home in one piece, Gus Pike."

"Sorry this an' sorry that, thank you, thank you, thank you, buncha hogwash!" piped Jo Pitts from the corner. All eyes turned to stare at the insolent girl. "Sure wish ya'd all quit yakkin' an figger out whatcher doin' with me!"

"I know what *I'd* do with you," snapped Aunt Janet, "but it's against the law."

"Miss King, if you don't mind my stickin' my two cents' worth in..." said Gus, looking directly at Hetty.

"Go ahead, Gus, speak your piece."

"Well, I'd like to say somethin' on Jo's behalf."

"I can't think of a thing I'd say on her behalf!" was Janet King's quick response. "I'd lock her up and throw away the key!"

"I know it," acknowledged Gus. "But ya gotta think what Jo had in her life. Not much, that's sure an' certain!" He looked around the table as the image of Jo's lonely childhood sank in. "She had nothin'. An' nobody." His dark eyes burned with earnest conviction. "Heck, Miss King, I was the same. I wouldn't know nothin' about nothin' if it weren't fer you makin' me go to school an' helpin' me haul myself up by the bootstraps!"

"Now, Gus," murmured Hetty, "don't compare yourself with this...creature. You were always a boy who tried your best, no matter what the situation."

"Yeah, but if you hadn't picked me outta the garbage heap an' taught me to be a gen'leman, I mighta ended up Lord knows where." He swallowed hard, trying to find the words to express his feelings. "Sendin' Jo Pitts to prison ain't gonna help her. It'll make her hard an' mean."

"Harder and meaner," corrected Janet.

"Sendin' her back where she come from ain't gonna help neither," advised Gus.

Hetty listened thoughtfully. More than anyone else at that kitchen table, Gus Pike knew about hard beginnings. Still, Gus Pike rose from the "garbage heap," as he so aptly put it, and ended up earning the respect of not just the King family, but all of Avonlea.

Hetty wavered. She glanced at Jo Pitts and her heart sank. Was it possible that given the same opportunities, Jo Pitts could become a sterling citizen, admired and respected by all? Hetty huddled under her blanket deep in thought, uncomfortably aware of Janet King's accusing stare. Still, there were those who had thought Gus Pike wouldn't make the grade either. And if Hetty hadn't persisted, why, perhaps he'd be the one crouched in her kitchen corner with a bag full of stolen silver, instead of Jo Pitts!

"What d'ya say, Miss King?"

Hetty knew Gus was waiting for her reply, and she heaved a great sigh. This was certainly a problem to test the wisdom of King Solomon. On one hand there was Gus Pike recommending mercy. On the other, there was Janet recommending the long arm of the law. Now, Gus might be a man of few words, thought Hetty, but in her experience, his ideas came straight from the heart and were grounded in good old-fashioned common sense. Hadn't Shakespeare himself said that mercy "droppeth like the gentle rain from heaven"? She racked her brain to think of a similar quotation from the Bible. Surely there was something. Why, the minister was forever rattling on about mercy...

"Mercy sakes !" cried Janet. "Gus Pike has asked you the same question three times. Are you sure that swim didn't botch up your eardrums?"

Hetty looked at Janet oddly. The Lord sent signs from the strangest places! "I can hear just fine, thank you, Janet," she replied. Then, squaring her shoulders under the blanket, she turned to the sour-faced young girl who was still sitting cross-legged in the corner, awaiting the verdict.

"You're a bad apple, Jo Pitts," said a stern Hetty, "but maybe Gus Pike is right. Maybe what you need is a regular life, with regular meals and regular hours."

"And school..." added Olivia.

"School certainly. And a nice clean place to live!" said Hetty. She paused, then added brightly, "I know! You could stay at..." She looked around the table, seeking inspiration. "You could stay at Janet's!"

"I beg your pardon!" squawked Janet, choking on her tea. And Felix looked as miserable as if he'd been told to give up dessert for a month.

Jo's eyes, wide as soup bowls, ricocheted back and forth from Janet to Hetty.

"Gus Pike, thank you kindly for your advice," said Hetty, wisely averting all-out war, "but I think Janet and Olivia and I need to discuss this matter privately."

"Oh sure," agreed Gus. "I'll be headin' back to the lighthouse. Thanks fer the tea. An' if there's anythin' I can do, Miss King, jest send Sara to fetch me."

Gus donned his cap, casting a sympathetic look at Sara. Then he paused at the doorway, glancing down at Jo. "It ain't too late to change your ways, Jo Pitts."

Jo looked stonily away, refusing to meet his frank and honest gaze. Gus shook his head, nodded Hetty's way and took his leave.

Hetty wasted no time evicting three more pairs of ears from the kitchen debate. "Felix King," she ordered, with a touch of the old firmness returning to her voice, "I think it's time you were seeing to your chores." Felix was more than happy to make his escape. "And, Sara, why don't you go to your room and freshen up? Take Jo with you, and for heaven's sake, keep an eye on her while Janet and Olivia and I talk this over *peacefully*." This last was accompanied by a glare at Janet, who was huffily pouring herself another cup of tea.

"Yes, Aunt Hetty" was Sara's response. "Come on Jo, let's go."

"*Yes, Aunt Hetty?*" hissed an astounded Jo Pitts, mimicking Sara's obedient tones. "She jest asks, an ya *do it*, without givin' her no lip, no nothin'?"

"Hush!" whispered Sara, glancing back at her three aunts, who were gathered around the kitchen table to determine Jo Pitts's fate. "For once in your life," she advised Jo, hauling her out of the kitchen and up the stairs, "please, I beg of you, quit while you're ahead!"

Hetty put her finger to her lips to silence Janet, who was exploding with anger. The three of them waited until they heard the sound of Sara's and Jo's footsteps scampering up the

stairs, and the bedroom door opening and closing. Satisfied that their conversation could now
be conducted privately, Hetty nodded to Janet,
who was itching to speak her piece.

"How could you *dream* of suggesting she
come live with me?" she cried indignantly. "I
wouldn't let her in my house if my life
depended on it! Let her stay with Olivia!"

"With *me?*" exclaimed Olivia, setting her
teacup down with a clatter. She looked at
Hetty pleadingly. "Oh heavens, what would
Jasper say?"

"Whatever it was, he'd take a long time
saying it," commented Hetty dryly.

"He couldn't handle Jo Pitts!" cried Olivia,
blanching at the very thought of that thieving
little pickpocket creating havoc in the Dale
honeymoon cottage. Dear Jasper needed peace
and quiet for his inventions. He could never
tolerate the commotion, let alone the prospect
of expensive gadgets simply disappearing into
Jo Pitts's loot bag! "Why can't she stay with
you, Hetty?" asked Olivia brightly.

This time it was Hetty's turn to be appalled.
"M-me?" she stammered, suddenly flustered.

"I think that's a brilliant idea!" said Janet, seizing on the opportunity to turn the tables on Hetty.

"No! I've had enough of that child to last a lifetime!" insisted Hetty. "Janet King," she said heatedly, "I am the eldest and it's my decision. She stays with you."

Janet stared at her. "Over my dead body!" she shrieked, setting her teacup down with such force that it cracked in two.

"That was my very best china!" scolded Hetty.

"Hetty! Janet! Please! We have a problem to solve!" cried Olivia.

"Mind your own business, Olivia!" hissed Janet. "And you see here, Hetty King!" she continued vehemently. "You can't push me around!"

"I'm not pushing, I'm suggesting!"

"Suggest all you want!" sputtered Janet, rising to her feet and groping for her hat. "But I'm leaving. And remember, if that dreadful child moves into my house, we're all *moving out!*"

Chapter Eighteen

While Jo Pitts eyed her warily from the bed, Sara wandered around the pretty bedroom in a state of wonderment, tidying up some of the mess that Jo had made and touching one thing after another—the daintily embroidered pillows, the lace curtains fluttering at the window, the ruffled chintz dressing table."Everything is so beautiful!" she murmured. "How could I ever have dreamed of running away?"

"Don't look at me," Jo said shrugging. "I just went along for the ride."

"That's not entirely true," said Sara, scrubbing her fingernails at the washbowl. She sat down at the dressing table and glanced at her reflection in the shattered mirror.

"Good grief!" she murmured. "I look a sight!" Horrified at her tangled hair, she picked up her silver-handled brush and began to tidy herself. "Let me remind you," Sara said, glancing back at Jo, who was wincing each time Sara yanked at a tangle, "this whole thing was your idea as much as mine, Jo Pitts."

"So what're ya bellyachin' about, then?" mumbled Jo.

Sara sighed and turned to Jo. "Because I have a bone to pick with you," she said evenly. "Yes, it's true we made a deal to switch places, but you never warned me about Buck Hogan and the pickpockets."

Jo guffawed loudly. "That ain't my fault! I never knew where you was goin'. How was I supposed to know you'd end up in their clutches? Anyhow, I got the worst of the bargain," she muttered ruefully. "You never warned me about Hetty King."

Sara paused to consider this. "Somehow one doesn't seem as bad as the other."

"They ain't," agreed Jo Pitts. "Hetty's worse."

"Nonsense!" said Sara. "Aunt Hetty's a pussycat next to Buck Hogan! I can tell you one thing—I wouldn't trade places with you again for all the tea in China!"

"Same here!" said Jo vehemently. "I've had enough o' this place!"

"But I thought you'd love it here" was Sara's surprised reply.

"Yeah. Well, I did at first. Especially the eats." Jo looked wistfully around the room. "An' when I first laid eyes on this room, I thought I musta died and went to heaven!"

"There," said Sara softly, "you see? It wasn't so bad after all!"

"But it was!" insisted Jo. "The room's pretty...but it's a prison. The four walls...an' the ol' bat orderin' me around night an' day."

"Don't call her names. She was only trying to look after you."

"Well, I ain't used to it. I missed bein' free."

"And I missed being safe," said Sara quietly.

The two girls looked at one another, for the very first time understanding the real difference between them.

Just then, Hetty's voice rang out. "Sara? Jo?" she called from downstairs. "Would you kindly come back down, please."

Impulsively Sara rose from her dressing table and took Jo's hand in hers. "Jo, I know it hasn't been easy, but wouldn't you like to give it another try?"

"Give what another try? Trading places?" Jo yanked her hand away in horror.

"No," said Sara gently. "We wouldn't trade. This time I'd stay, too."

"You mean...you an' me, together, we'd live here?" said an astounded Jo Pitts.

"Yes," said Sara. "I don't want you to leave. I found out now how hard it is to live by your wits on the streets, being forced to steal just to survive." She sat down beside Jo and continued earnestly, "Please, Jo, don't go back. I know Aunt Hetty will let you stay here. Things could turn out differently this time."

For one single, solitary moment, Jo Pitts seemed to soften. Was it possible? Could she ever forget the old ways, the wild freedom, the thrill of danger waiting around every corner? Gus Pike said it wasn't too late to change. She looked at Sara, who waited so quietly, so earnestly for an answer. Nobody in Jo's whole life had ever made such a kind offer. Jo's eyes shone. Salty tears brimmed and spilled over. Then quickly she brushed them away, lest Sara get the wrong impression.

"Naw," she said gruffly, hiding her emotions,

"it ain't no use. I don't fit." Very slowly, she removed the cameo pin from her blouse and handed it to Sara. "Here," she muttered, "this here's yours. We made the bet I could take your place, but I figger I lost."

Sara looked at the delicately carved cameo, remembering the very shop in Italy where her father had taken her to browse for gifts. It had been a perfect summer afternoon, the sun shining like a golden corona over the magical city of Firenze, and they had wandered onto a bridge of tiny, exquisite jewelry shops. She recalled admiring the little cameo and her father purchasing it as a memento of their journey. She was so fortunate. She had so many souvenirs and warm memories, each and every one a treasure...and Jo Pitts had none.

Ever so gently, she pinned the cameo back on Jo's blouse. "You keep it," she said, "to remember me by."

"*Girls!*" Hetty's voice rang out from downstairs. "No dilly-dallying!"

"We'd better go," said Sara.

"Yeah." Jo's voice was husky with emotion. "Uh...why don't you go on ahead," she said, looking towards the open window. "I'll be down...in a minute."

Sara glanced at the window, and in her heart of hearts she knew what Jo was going to do. "Very well." An understanding passed between the two girls. "I'll see you downstairs, Jo."

"Sure. Downstairs."

Sara walked to the door and paused for one last look back at Jo.

"Jo...?" she said hesitantly, hopefully.

Jo shook her head. "Don't say no more, Sara. I ain't you and you ain't me. An' that's the end of it."

Sara smiled. Then she left the room, closing the door quietly behind her.

For a brief moment, Jo sat on the bed looking around her at the room she had grown to love. She stared at the closed door as though a bittersweet portion of her life was over and done with. "So long, Sara," she murmured sadly.

Then, with a sigh, she bounced off the bed, grabbed the silver-handled brush and comb from Sara's dresser, hiked up her skirt and dropped them into her petticoat pocket.

"Jo Pitts!" hollered Hetty. "Do you expect us to wait all day?"

"Don't hold yer breath," muttered Jo to herself, "'cuz I ain't comin'!"

With that, she ran to the window, raised the sash to the top and climbed out onto the ledge, shinnying down the trellis like a bolt of lightning.

"That girl is slow as molasses in January!" declared Hetty King as she inspected Sara's fingernails for cleanliness. "Whatever is keeping her?"

"I don't know," murmured Sara, glancing over Hetty's shoulder out the kitchen window. She smiled softly to herself, for there was Jo Pitts, racing across the yard, heading for the open meadows. Suddenly she stopped and ran back. Sara's heart skipped a beat. Had she changed her mind? But no, Jo was running towards the clothesline where the laundry flapped in the breeze.

Sara concealed a gasp as Jo grabbed a dimity blouse and lace-trimmed skirt off the line, hiked up her own skirt and shoved the two items into her ample petticoat pockets. In a flash, Jo lifted her eyes and caught Sara looking at her through the window. A smile lit up Jo's face. Sara smiled back.

"Whatever are you grinning at, girl?" asked Hetty. "You look like the cat that swallowed the canary!"

"It's nothing, Aunt Hetty."

Over Hetty's shoulder, Sara saw Jo wave a last goodbye before she raced off, tearing across the meadows towards the red dirt road, then disappeared around a bend in the road, free at last!

Sara turned to her aunt and took her hand in her own. "Did I tell you, Aunt Hetty, how very happy I am to be home?"

Skylark takes you on the...

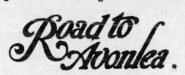

Based on the Sullivan Films production adapted from the novels of
LUCY MAUD MONTGOMERY

☐ THE JOURNEY BEGINS, Book #1 $3.99/NCR   48027-8

☐ THE STORY GIRL EARNS HER NAME, Book #2 $3.99/NCR   48028-6

☐ SONG OF THE NIGHT, Book #3 $3.99/NCR   48029-4

☐ THE MATERIALIZING OF DUNCAN McTAVISH, Book #4 $3.99/NCR   48030-8

☐ QUARANTINE AT ALEXANDER ABRAHAM'S, Book #5 $3.99/NCR   48031-6

☐ CONVERSATIONS, Book #6 $3.99/NCR   48032-4

☐ AUNT ABIGAIL'S BEAU, Book #7 $3.99/NCR   48033-2

☐ MALCOLM AND THE BABY, Book #8 $3.99/NCR   48034-0

☐ FELICITY'S CHALLENGE, Book #9 $3.99/NCR   48035-9

☐ THE HOPE CHEST OF ARABELLA KING, Book #10 $3.99/NCR   48036-7

☐ NOTHING ENDURES BUT CHANGE, Book #11 $3.99/NCR   48037-5

☐ SARA'S HOMECOMING, Book #12 $3.99/NCR   48038-3

☐ AUNT HETTY'S ORDEAL, Book #13 $3.99/NCR   48039-1

☐ OF CORSETS AND SECRETS AND TRUE,
TRUE LOVE, Book #14 $3.99/NCR   48040-5

☐ OLD QUARRELS, OLD LOVE, Book #15 $3.99/NCR   48041-3

☐ FAMILY RIVALRY, #16 $3.99/NCR   48042-1

*ROAD TO AVONLEA is the trademark of Sullivan Films Inc.

BANTAM BOOKS
Dept. SK50, 2451 South Wolf Road, Des Plaines, IL 60018

Please send me the items I have checked above. I am enclosing
$_____ (please add $2.50 to cover postage and handling).
Send check or money order, no cash or C.O.D.'s please.

MR/MS _____

ADDRESS _____

CITY/STATE _____ ZIP _____

Please allow four to six weeks for delivery.
Prices and availability subject to change without notice.   SK50-8/93